VENTRILOQUIST

2020

KEV CARTER

PLEASE VISIT MY WEBSITE

www.fancyacoffee.wix.com/kev-carter-books

CHAPTER ONE

The office was not clean but it was well worked, the place had been decorated a long time

ago and from that day on, just touched up occasionally.

The walls had posters and framed programs decorating them from performers and acts from the stage and screen, most gone and long forgotten.

He sat there, calm and expressionless, a large suitcase by his side, he was dressed sensibly and tidy, there didn't seem like anything special about him and no one would pay him a second look in the street.

That was just how he liked it, he sat on a wooden chair and waited patiently, his right hand resting on the suitcase and looking forward.

He had been there almost an hour now and had no response from the office in front of him. His appointment was for 2.00pm, he had arrived at 1.45pm. The young annoying girl the agent called a secretary had told him to wait and then gone into the office. She was still in there, he had heard giggling and the odd moan. He paid it no attention at this time but it had been locked away in his memory. He looked down at the suitcase and then back at the door.

Another twenty minutes passed before the door opened and a bitchy looking young girl came out adjusting her hair as she did, this was the secretary of sorts who ignored him and walked out the other door. He looked at the agent's door which had been left open, he could see inside an empty desk, a moment later a large overweight man came from the side and sat at this desk, he looked up and caught sight of him, he gestured him to come in as he looked at his watch. Calmly he stood and took the suitcase in with him, he closed the door behind him and stood in front of this obnoxious man, who looked up and then looked him up and down.

"Ok let me see what you have got, I am a busy man so don't be offended if I send you on your way, what you have to understand is I have seen it all and heard it all, if you have nothing special then you might as well leave now, I have managed the best and know what works and what doesn't." His voice was unfriendly and his body language matched it perfectly. He leaned back in his chair and took a deep breath clasped his hands behind his head and waited, the sweat stains were under his arms and the odor followed.

"Thank you for seeing me, I think I will show you something that you will be very interested in and maybe not seen before"

"What is your name by the way?" The agent snapped.

"Geoff"

"Do you not have a stage name; bloody Geoff is not going to get you anywhere is it?"

Smiling, Geoff placed the suitcase on the floor and carefully opened it, he pulled out the perfect looking dummy and held it in his right hand as he stood up straight again. He placed his foot on the small wooden chair in front of him and sat the dummy on his knee; he put his hand in the hole in the back and got his hand on the controls ready.

It was a pristine condition ventriloquist dummy, wide eye's, just oversize head but not too much to stand out, dressed in a suit and bright polished shoes, the overall effect looked proficient and professional.

"Let me stop you there before you begin, I have seen these acts before and to be honest they are dead as a dodo, drinking water as you say the alphabet, trying to get the audience to concentrate on the doll instead of your mouth movement, it is all old stuff and has been seen before, you have to be very skilled and have something new for it to work so you better be good and I mean fucking good"

Smiling Geoff took a deep breath and looked the agent straight in the eye, the doll seemed to click into life and the eyes moved round the head turned to inspect the room then it fixed its gaze on the agent, for a moment it just stared at him then the expression changed and the eye brows lifted and the mouth opened.

"Let me introduce myself because it is me you will want not him" the dummy spoke in a very audible voice and there was no muffle or distortion whatsoever, just a very sensible but little

4

menacing tone. Geoff's mouth never moved a fraction and he was still and silent as the dummy spoke.

The dummy smiled at the agent, then the head turned to Geoff who looked back at it and smiled, the dummy smiled back and then looked at the agent once more.

"Get on with the act, I am a busy man" He said pulling his hands back onto the desk as he leaned forward.

"Ok, ok let's get on with it, can you please give this man a deck of cards Geoff" the dummy instructed and from nowhere Geoff produced a deck of cards in his left hand and threw then on the table in front of the agent.

"Open the pack, see it is a new pack and then shuffle them," the dummy insisted, this was done without any enthusiasm, "Ok now you pick a card, and place it on the table in front of you," this was done as instructed.

"I know you are not yet impressed but just wait and see" the dummy did all the talking and Geoff said nothing. His mouth never twitched, and there was not even movement in his throat, the agent watched and noticed this and knew this man was very good.

"Ok your card was what?" the dummy asked baring its teeth in a macabre smile.

"Three of diamonds" The agent said looking at Geoff and trying to see any movement whatsoever in his throat or lips.

"Turn the card over then" The dummy insisted.

This was done and it was blank, the agent looked up quickly, he knew it was a trick but had not seen it done at this distance before, he looked at Geoff.

"Magic with a dummy?" the agent said.

"Look at the cards please" the dummies voice had become stern and serious.

Flicking through the rest of the deck he was amazed they were all the three of diamonds, he picked at them and rubbed them to see if they were trick cards in anyway, he had just shuffled them and he had just looked at them seeing they were a normal deck.

"Cute trick, is that your best one?"

"Oh no sir we do a song and dance act too, but let me ask you to take something from your pocket and I will show you some magic"

"You need some rapport between you and the dummy, some interaction, banter, you need to speak to each other" the Agent insisted.

"We will come to that later" Geoff said.

"Yes we will. I do not like him speaking when I do" the dummy came back with perfectly.

"I will let him impress you, then we will go into a comedy act as well" Geoff began.

"I am the one who impresses you see and then he comes back with some jokes" the dummy carried on to perfection.

"We have many routines, some funny, some amazing, and some that will just leave you for dead" Geoff smiled.

"Right, but before that, take something from your pocket and let me show you some bloody magic" the dummy insisted looking at the Agent intensely.

"What do you want from my pocket?"

"Any fucking thing, just take something out?" it snapped.

"Calm down and watch your language" Geoff said looking at his dummy.

Reaching into his pocket the agent took out his wallet and placed it on the desk in front of him. He looked up at Geoff and waited.

"Hey, it's me who is doing the fucking trick" the dummy spat.

Turning his attention to the dummy the agent stared into its eyes.

"Ok that's good, look at me and I will show you some real magic"

They stared at each other for a moment then the dummy let out a hideous laugh and rocked back and forth on Geoff's knee.

"What, what is so fucking funny?" the agent snapped at Geoff.

"Ok first let me open your wallet, looking down he saw the

wallet was opened and spread out on the desk, he looked up at Geoff aghast, sticking out of the inside pocket was a playing card, he took this out and turned it over. It was the three of diamonds.

"Let me close the wallet for you" The dummy laughed and the wallet snapped shut by itself, the agent threw himself back in the chair and the startled look on his face caused the dummy to mockingly laugh at him.

"What the fuck is going on" the agent demanded.

"Well this is just the start, it gets really good in a bit" the dummy said turning its head to Geoff who turned his head and they looked at each other. Then they both looked at the wide eyed and slightly nervous agent who was backing into his chair as far as he could.

"Are you OK? This is just the start, or is it too much for you?" The dummy asked calmly

"You are not moving your lips, there is nothing there whatsoever, that is not a fucking dummy is it" the agent came forward in his chair looking at the dummy in front of him, looking back into his eyes.

"Boo" the dummy shouted and the eyes opened wide and the teeth were bared into a snarl as the face became evil looking for a moment, the agent jumped back in fear but the dummy stayed motionless.

Geoff took the dummy off his knee and placed it on the table laid flat on its back, he undid some Velcro fastening round the arms and pulled these off and he did the same with the legs. Then the head was pulled out from the neck to revel a wooden ventriloquist dummy, lifeless and in pieces.

He sat down on the chair in front of him and watched the agent carefully prod the wooden dummy on his desk. He picked up a leg and tapped it, seeing it was made of wood, he prodded the chest and felt it was also solid wood.

He was amazed at the skill of this man's Ventriloquist skill, he had no idea how he had done the trick with the wallet but he saw the wallet move by itself he was sure of that.

"You are good, son, I will give you that, very good, but it takes a lot more than just being clever to make it big, you need help and I can give you that help, you were right to come to me" The agent smiled for the first time, but it did not change Geoff's still expression.

"What about me?" the voice came from the dummy on his desk.

"You throw your voice very well I must say you are good at this" The agent said looking at Geoff then the dummy and back to Geoff.

"Well it took a lot of understanding to be able to do it, it took me a long time to be able to express it and tame it, and understand it" Geoff said.

"What do you mean tame it? I need you in control you have to be in control"

"I am in control, perfect control at all times, you are in for a treat and a real show of magic soon. Believe me, something that has never been done before."

"You make me nervous I don't know why, but you do" The agent suddenly put up his guard and looked deep into Geoff's eyes but saw nothing, nothing like emotion at all.

"Well I know you are a busy man and must see a lot of people, I know you have a casting couch and I know you abuse young girls, I know you use people and mercilessly ruin lives, I know much more about you then you can imagine with your narrow, bigoted, selfish, pathetic and filthy mind."

Geoff had become frightening to him, he could not look him in the eye anymore and turned away, he tried to stand but could not he fought to get out of his chair but could not move.

"Get out; get the fuck out of my office"

"As you can see, like I said, I am in control and you will now see some real magic."

The agent's heart raced, he was petrified, he could not move and he could do nothing about it. Looking at the dummy on his desk he thought he saw movement. He looked again and his eyes widened, the left arm moved, it moved by its self, the fingers stretched out and the whole arm flinched. He stared at Geoff who was looking intensely back at him with a slight, evil smile on his face.

The arm twitched and the hand stretched out and pulled itself across the desk to the second arm, he watched as the arm moved and took hold of the other arm locking it back into place in the torso of the dummy, the second arm reached out and the dummy sat up, pulling the legs back into the joints and locking them into place. The legs and arms were now both locked in and the hands reached down for the head, lifting it up and slotting it back into the neck. The head quickly spun round and stared with wide eyes and mouth open in a snarl at the agent, who was paralyzed with fear as he witnessed the unbelievable spectacle in front of him. He gulped and swallowed looking back at Geoff.

"My young sister came to you some time ago, she was very talented, a superb singer, nice polite and very naïve, do you remember what you said to her?" Geoff asked him.

"Do you remember her?" The dummy shouted as its head shook in anger as it did so.

"No, no I don't know," The agent could not move he was riveted to his chair with fear and felt the wetness trickle down his leg as he wet himself.

"You said you would do your best for her, you said she would go far, you would take her under your wing, look after her" Geoff continued in a quiet composed voice.

"Please, what do you want?" shaking he could do nothing as he had never felt such fear or terror running through his bones. The dummy was staring at him and tilting its head to one side as it did, the menacing look it gave him sent him cold.

"She trusted you", Geoff continued, "and you abused her, Cynthia Bothemly is her name, you said you would get her a much better stage name, all she had to do was trust you, she was sixteen, just sixteen"

The face of the agent turned to confusion then his eyes widened as he remembered the girl and how he took advantage of her, he thought she was a run away and took full advantage of the situation as he always does.

The dummy turned its head and looked at Geoff for a moment, and then it spun back with a snapping sound to stare at the agent once again before saying.

"You took advantage, you abused and did so much damage you will never know you filthy bastard, I will be watching you and I will be coming for you." The laugh that followed was something that instantly imprinted itself on his mind and brain.

Geoff stood up, picked up the dummy and placed it back into the suitcase. He took the deck of cards from the desk and put these in his pocket as he looked down at the petrified man looking up at him from the chair.

"Don't call us, we will be calling on you" he said and with that he turned and left the office.

Silence followed and the shaking was uncontrollable. For a long minute he sat there looking at the door that was closed behind the man who had just left his office. Eventually he shouted out to his secretary.

"Emma, Emma in here now"

Moments later the young girl came in and walked to the desk looking very confused at her boss shaking in the chair with a wet stain on his pants.

"Yes sir?" she asked.

"The man who has just left with a dummy, suitcase whatever it was, did you see him, did you get his address and name, who was he?" he spluttered out the questions and waited impatiently for the answers.

"You have had no visitors all afternoon sir" she said confused somewhat.

"You showed the man in girl, what are you talking about, you took his details and made the appointment" he shouted.

"Please sir I am confused, there has been no one here all afternoon as I have not taken any bookings sir" the girl was genuinely upset and confused and he realized she must have been brain washed or something.

"Oh get out you silly little bitch, get out and stay out"

She rushed from the room crying and bewildered, upset and confused. He looked round and didn't know what to do, he remembered the girl Cynthia Bothemly. He remembered taking her to a hotel room with promises of stardom and important meetings with record producers. He remembered getting her drunk and raping her, he remembered her tears and how it turned him on even more when she fought him off, or at least tried to fight him off. This happened a long time ago and she just disappeared. He put it down to one more notch to his collection and paid it no more notice, he had sick friends who always would give him perfect alibis and had the security of some powerful people who scratched his back, in return for a supply of young hopefuls who would do anything for the chance of stardom.

He stood up and looked out of the window, searching the street outside; he turned and rubbed his mouth with the back of his hand. Breathing heavy he looked round then left the office, he stormed past the desk where the young girl was still sobbing, and he paid her no notice and dashed out of the door. He rushed to his car and got in. He checked the back seat and looked around like some crazed lunatic, checking every corner, every person he saw. The fear within him rose and he started the car. He pulled away and headed off down the street, looking in his mirror as he did.

He drove quickly his eyes searching everywhere as he did; he drove home and dashed into his modest house. Locking the door behind him he went into the living room going to the window and looked out of it, up and down the street, across his drive and everywhere he could see. He ran up stairs and got changed out of his clothes. He dashed about, packing a suitcase, just throwing things in. He came down stairs and into the living room, taking a bottle of whiskey from the side board he poured himself a glass, gulping it down straight away, he poured another one.

He went and sat down to try and steady himself a little. Had he just witnessed what he saw? Did he imagine it? Was he dreaming? The questions flooded into his head as he sat back into his chair and took a deep breath.

He tried to steady himself and then sighed out, he must be safe here, and no one could know where he lived. He had friends to stay with until it was over, he knew some people who could sort problems out and they always delivered. Nasty people who asked no questions and break limbs for a living, he would hire a few of these and would not be bothered again, yeah that is it, he would get this sorted out.

The thoughts made him feel better and he relaxed back blowing air out of his lungs and sighing. He sat up and rubbed his face then he saw it, a single card on his coffee table, the three of diamonds.

He froze and started to whimper uncontrollably not taking his eyes off the card on the table. He shook and felt the emptiness in his stomach.

"You see, what you do not realize is, we have been watching you for a long time, we know where you live, where you go, your habits your hideouts" it was the voice of the dummy and it was coming from the arm chair behind him.

He dare not look and could not muster the courage to stand.

"Please leave me alone" was all he could say in a weak scared voice.

"I bet those were her words exactly weren't they, please leave me alone, please stop, please it hurts, please do not hit me, please stop touching, please, please, please"

Geoff walked into the room, from where, he didn't see, he looked over to him but didn't move his head only his eyes.

Geoff looked at him with hate in his eyes, standing in front of him he just looked down and stayed motionless.

"What do you want? What can I do to make you go away?" the

agent pleaded. Geoff didn't speak it was the dummy that answered from the chair.

"What you did was disgusting, what you do is vile and degrading, you ruin people's lives and get away with it because you have powerful friends. Well every dummy has its day and today its mine" the laugh that followed chilled his blood and he shook even more.

Geoff went to the side and took the three quarter full bottle of whiskey, he came and put it in front of the agent, he signaled for him to take a drink of it. Nervously he did as he was instructed.

"Drink it all, the whole fucking bottle" Geoff demanded.

"All of it, you drink all of it" the voice from the chair added.

"I take it you got Cynthia drunk, I take it you slapped her about a bit too" Geoff said with anger in his voice. Without warning he slapped the agent across the face reeling him back in pain and surprise.

"Hurts, doesn't it?" The voice from the chair shouted out.

"Drink that fucking bottle now, you piece of shit" Geoff said loudly.

The bottle was drunk quickly and he almost made himself sick as he drank it, he gulped and retched a bit, but fear made him do it.

"All of it, you drink all of it" the voice screeched from the chair.

He coughed and spluttered but managed it eventually; Geoff took the bottle from him and placed it on the coffee table saying.

"You feel better now do you, more relaxed, a bit more helpless, more vulnerable, less able to resist?"

"More of the drunken, dirty, filthy pig you are" the voice shouted from the chair.

"Have you noticed the rapport we have now, more interaction wouldn't you say" Geoff added. He walked over to the side and took another bottle of whiskey and threw it at his helpless scared victim in front of him.

"Now you get to drink that one as well" the dummy laughed.

Shaking his head the agent tried to plead with Geoff but it was no good the bottle was thrust in front of him and he was made to drink it.

"I want that bottle drank as well, because I want you to feel as helpless and as scared as Cynthia did, do you remember what you did to her?"

"Drink, and don't spill a drop" the voice bellowed out from the arm chair in a mockingly way with a giggle and evil snarl.

"I will give you anything you want, money I can get you money" the agent pleaded once more, but nothing he could say would change anything that was obvious to him now.

"Promises, you are so good at making promises, but you don't deliver do you? You just manipulate and take advantage, you bully and hurt."

"You need to be taught a lesson you see" the voice from the chair rang in his ears.

"Drink the fucking whisky" Geoff shouted and stared with angry eyes at him.

The agent began to take drinks from the bottle, he was feeling sick, ill and he was petrified. The alcohol was taking effect and he could feel his ability to perform being taken from him, his body was not responding to what he wanted it to do. He took another mouthful and dribbled it down his front.

"Time to get the rope I think" the dummy said loudly.

"Rope?" the agent said slurring his speech as he did.

"Yes you must have some in fact I know you do, because you sometimes tie young girls up don't you, go and get the rope from your kitchen cupboard I will wait here, but don't be long.

"Don't keep us waiting now will you" the dummy added.

Without knowing why, the agent staggered to his feet, Geoff staring at him the entire time. Wobbling to the kitchen, he went to the cupboard and pulled out a rope, he felt sick and dizzy but by some strange force he did as he was commanded.

When he came back into the room, Geoff had the dummy on his knee again and they both looked at him, it was the same pose he had taken in the office earlier.

"Tie a loop in the end of the rope and feed the other end through it, throw that over the wooden beam above you" the dummy commanded.

It was done, swaying on the spot the agent waited.

"Take another drink" Geoff insisted.

As he did he watched the dummy staring at him with wide eyes and a grin on its face.

"Take a chair and place it under the rope, then stand on it, wrap the rope round your neck tight, then tie it round the rest of the rope so you are secure" the dummy's voice was mesmerizing and had to be obeyed.

This was done, and the agent was drunk helpless and very unsteady on the chair. The rope was tight round his neck and secured well.

"What you have to realise is, when you hang yourself you have to do it right, a quick snapping action as you reach the bottom of the rope and the neck breaks, but if not, you will hang there and choke to death, it is very unpleasant and painful" the dummy informed him.

"Please, let me go" the agent managed to say eventually.

"Did Cynthia say them words to you while you raped her, got her so drunk she didn't know what the hell was happening, did you slap her about a bit just for the fun of it"

Geoff asked him as he wobbled precariously on the chair.

"He is not looking very well Geoff" the dummy said turning its head to look at Geoff then spinning round back to the agent again.

"My sister never recovered from what you did to her, too shy, too scared to tell anyone she became a shell, empty, a shadow of her bubbly joyful self. You took her life and her dreams from her. Used her for your own gratification and sexual pleasure, well today she is going to be revenged, today you are going to die and a painful death at that" Geoff told him while he watched him slip and wobble on the chair. The rope was tight and felt threatening and he was scared, the whiskey had made him unstable and he began to wet himself again.

"You are fucking disgusting do you know that" the dummy said shaking its head.

"You've not even said sorry, never asked about her, never shown any remorse or regret, all you have done is offered me money and pleaded for yourself, you selfish bastard" Geoff said as he watched him cry and stagger to one side, the rope tightening on his neck.

He reached up and tried to untie it, he was desperate and struggled to undo the rope, he lost balance and slipped to one side the chair followed and it leaned over on two legs. A cry of terror and fear came from him as his weight shifted and he miss footed the chair completely. It fell over and he dropped the rope tight round his neck strangling him, he choked and reached up trying to take his weight but he was too drunk and had no coordination or strength to do so. He began to kick out as his throat burned and the pain tore into his neck, he was gasping for air as the rope choked him. His whole body swung violently catching sight of the dummy laughing at him as he turned round and started to lose consciousness. The air supply was cut off as he frantically reached and grabbed for the rope but it was no good, he was choking. His tongue was swelling and filling his mouth, his eyes bulged in their sockets with the pressure.

Geoff watched until he was still, his body turning on the rope round his neck, his body limp, the life choked from him.

Geoff looked at the dummy and the dummy looked at him saying

"It was too good for him. It should have taken longer"

"Well at least, he will not be abusing anyone else will he" Geoff answered.

"We should be on the stage you and me; we would bring the house down"

Geoff didn't say anything as he walked from the room and then the house, unseen and

Unnoticed. The body was left hanging there slowly turning and swaying, he looked hideous

And smelt terrible, but then again people were always used to him being disgusting.

Walking calmly down the street with his suitcase in his hand Geoff got into his car he had parked several streets away. Putting the suitcase on the front seat and opening it to reveal the dummy laid there staring up. He drove off and headed home.

"That was too good for him, we should have done more" The dummy said.

"It was easy; I told you it would be, justice has been served there, and we need to move onto the others now" Geoff talked to his dummy like it was a person sat next to him, it was natural and the dummy returned just as natural. But it was not always there in person, the voice of the dummy was always with him. He had learned to control it, and learned to understand what it all meant the bond, the unbreakable trust. He sighed and turned into a busy road and headed away going a little faster in traffic has he did.

"I was impressed with your hypnotic skill with that annoying bitch secretary by the way, didn't tell you before but you mastered that really well Geoff"

"Thank you, she was easy to manipulate actually, very weak would have been harder to have hypnotized a gold fish I think, she will remember nothing about us" Geoff said pleased he managed it all the same.

CHAPTER TWO

It was several days before the hung body was found, a police investigation was set up, it looked like suicide but there was no note. The police interviewed a lot of people, they found out a lot of things and the investigation went off in a lot of different directions, but ultimately it was a suicide. Some powerful people with powerful and influential friends were kept out of the investigation and it was closed sooner than it should have been. He was drunk he was not doing well in business and some shady dealings left him no choice, he got drunk and he committed suicide, case closed.

But the case would not be closed for a long time yet, not in Geoff's eyes, he knew of a few others who needed taking care of, but they would not be easy, not as easy as this one, this one was wide open and vulnerable. But the others were going to be harder and have a lot more protection and be very shrewd.

It was early morning and Geoff got out of bed and went to have a shower. He made some breakfast and then the dummy finally spoke to him. It was sat in a chair, its own chair, in the living room of the modest apartment.

"So when do we get going with what needs to be done?" It asked

"Soon, I am still trying to figure out the best way to do it, we had to watch that fat Bastard for weeks don't forget the others will not be as easy" Geoff sat down with a bowl of cereal at the kitchen area table.

"Why are you sat in there, I am in here?"

"Because this is where the breakfast table is you dummy" Geoff said eating a mouthful off his spoon.

"What the hell is wrong with you?"

"Leave me alone a bit, I am not feeling too good"

There was silence after that, the dummy said nothing and didn't move. Geoff got ready and headed off to work. The apartment was silent and still. It would be until Geoff came back later that evening. But he went to his parent's house first before going home; he often did visit after work to see his sister. The house was a modest place on a modest estate, he had grown up here and his parents bought it from new, they would die here and never leave, they have told him many times. His mother always made him a good large meal when he visited and today was no exception. He went in and took off his shoes placing them on a little carpet by the door put there especially for this purpose. The place was spotless and tidy nothing out of place and a place for everything. His mother was a tall thin woman who had grey hair and looked younger then she actually was. She came and gave him a hug closing her eyes for a moment has he hugged her back.

"Good to see you son" she said in a very articulated voice.

"Good to see you mum you are looking well, where's dad?" he asked as they walk through the hallway and into a spacious living room decorated with years of memories and souvenirs from their life and travels, different photos of children at different ages.

"He is in the shed, again, not sure what the hell he is doing but it keeps him out of my way"

"You can't live without him and you know it" Geoff smiled at her and looked up his smile fading has he did.

"You can go up, your food won't be ready for about half hour, I knew you would want to talk to her for a little before we ate" His mother said with a smile but worried look in her eyes.

Geoff hugged her again and went up stairs he knocked on the bedroom door then walked in. It was a girl's room. Decorated like it was a ten year olds maybe, but sat on the bed putting a little outfit on a doll was a young woman, she was around eighteen dressed in a flowery dress and with her hair up in a bun. She was dressing the plastic doll in her hands her head tilted slightly to the side as she did. She looked up as he walked in. putting the doll down instantly she looked at him with a pale expression. He walked over and sat on the bed next to her. He looked her in the eye and then they hugged.

"Remember what we talked about, that thing you never like talking about?" he whispered

27

She turned away and shook her head, her face breaking into a cry as she tried to hold back her tears. He took her in his arms again and looked her in the eye. She sniffed up and stopped crying. She had learned to control it a little bit, but it would never be right again.

"Yes I remember" she said softly.

"Well I know you have never told anyone, and you never need too, and also you never need worry about it again. Do you understand what I mean, remember what we said and what I said to you about taking the painful thing away so it could never hurt you or anyone again?"

"Yes I remember, I do" she nodded her head not taking her eyes from his.

"Well it is gone, and always will be gone, it will never come back it can't. Do you understand? "He smiled at her and kissed her softly on the forehead.

She hugged him and began to sob quietly he held her close and comforted her, the way he always has and always will do. The way he promised her he would and now he hoped she might start to recover a little better she had retracted into herself so much. He was the only one who knew what had happened, the only one except for Dummy.

Later at the dinner table they all sat eating a large well made roast dinner. Dad who was a large man at the head of the table mum at the other end opposite and Geoff and his sister at each side also opposite. They ate in silence for a short while until his mum spoke.

"How was your day at work Geoff anything happen?"

"Same shit different day mum, bloody place is corrupt from the top down"

"Most factories are these days, all they are bothered about is making money" his Dad said not looking up and stuffing the food into his mouth at a fast rate.

"Yeah, I have been there over twenty years and they don't give a shit, I am being told what to do by a bloody woman who doesn't know her arse from her elbow, fucking bitch"

"Geoff, please, not at the dinner table and stop being sexist" his mother told him,

"I am not being sexist, she is a bitch, been given a little power she is abusing and it's gone straight to her head, it's her way or no way"

"Yep, should never put women in charge of men, it's a fact" his dad said chewing his full mouth of food swallowing and then taking a long drink of water from his glass.

"That is sexist, you need to see things from every point of view" his mum defended.

"She has no idea how to do the job, never done the job, but she is telling men who have done the job for over twenty years they are doing it wrong, they have to do it her way, she will not listen to anyone. She rears up as soon as you say anything she makes enemies of people who could actually help her and she lies to upper management to justify her job" Geoff told her.

"Yeah, would never of had that in my day, people in charge knew what the hell they were talking about, not some twat who knows fuck all" his dad said nodding his head.

"Language, please what is wrong with you two tonight?" His mother said looking at them

"It is fact love, there is too many people in charge who should not be, it never would of happened in my day, no, supervisors and the such came from the shop floor, up through the ranks. They had respect from the workforce because they use to be the workforce and didn't forget that either" he filled his mouth again with food and looked at Geoff for support and acknowledgment.

"Exactly, they just kiss ass above them and treat them below them like shit, to many people in charge who should not be in charge. Who then set people on they can manipulate and control, who are kiss asses and so on, the whole structure is weakened and fucked" Geoff said glancing over to his dad who was agreeing with a nodding head.

"Well if you hate it so much why not leave?" his mum said

"There are no jobs out there mum, I don't have a piece of paper saying I am smart from a college or university. No one wants to give you a chance anymore"

"Yeah not like that in my day, you walked into a job and they set you on if you were no good they kicked you out the door, if you were any good you had a job, real people real workers looking after the real people and workers, they are scared to death to say anything these days" His dad said drinking more water from his glass.

"Yep politically correctness, ruins everything, you can't say what you want anymore and can't say certain things because you offend certain people" Geoff added

"Oh yeah, not like my day you called a spade a spade, it's our country and we fought a bloody war to keep it free and safe, I say what I want when I want, fuck em"

"Alright that is enough, too much language at this table" his mum said to them both.

There was a silence then as they all ate their food, when finished dad went back into his shed and Cynthia went back to her room. Geoff was going to help with the dishes but his mum would not hear of it. A short time later he left saying good bye to everyone before he did.

He was full, it always was good food from his mums table, he drove steady and the night had drawn in. he pulled up and locked his car then went up the stairs to let himself into the apartment block where he lived.

Dummy was still sat in the chair he had not moved, Geoff threw his keys onto a small table by the door and went and got changed. He came back into the kitchen just off from the main room dressed in loose and comfortable pants and tee shirt. He sat down on the settee and looked over at the dummy. The head spun round with a click and the mouth dropped open then it said.

"How was the family, all good I hope?"

"Yeah they doing well, dad as great as ever" he sighed out and stretched.

"Cynthia, did you tell her, how was she?" the dummy asked blinking its eyes.

"I told her she understood, that is all I could see within her, what else is there for her to say?"

"Well at least we and now she knows the Bastard is dead"

"Yeah at least there is that" Geoff stretched out again and relaxed into the settee.

"So let us work on the next, she is a bitch and needs taking down" the dummy said round then back again to look at Geoff.

"She is not going to be easy, now that fat Bastard is dead they will all be on guard, we have to take what we know about her then work off that I think"

"Ok, we know she is a known associate of his and obviously knows about the little racket he had going, young girls vulnerable and weak, possibly drug addicted, take advantage of them and rather leave them for dead or use them in the sex trade"

"Cynthia was so bloody lucky in one way you know, it could have easily gone the other way and we never saw her again and never knew" Geoff put his hands on his head and breathed out exaggeratedly.

"Well we did and she got safe, but if she is lucky I don't know? I want revenge and I want this bitch to suffer, not fast like the last one but I want it to go on and want her to feel the shit scared fear she has made the young girls, and boys, feel" the mouth opened and the eyes blinked. Geoff looked over at the dummy.

"Maybe we could leave it we have got the one responsible and got away with it"

"What, what the fuck you saying, no, no, no" the dummy ratted where it sat and shook its head, the eyes were wide and the arms came up and down in a tantrum several time.

"Calm down, I was just saying" Geoff sighed out and tilted his head back closing his eyes.

"Don't you forget, do not forget, ever" the dummy said staring at him.

"How can I, you will never let me" Geoff said not opening his eyes.

"Why should I, we made a deal and it can never be broken, do you not remember the time before, do you not remember what was said, what was done?"

"Of course I do, it is with me every single day" Geoff got up and went to the kitchen and put the kettle on. While he was waiting for the water to boil he got a cup and put a tea bag in it, then took some milk for the fridge and waited. When he had made his tea he came back into the room, the dummy was now on the settee and staring at him. So Geoff going over and Sitting in the chair he took a sip of his hot tea.

"Ok, so how shall we do it, it is going to take some doing not getting caught on this one, because when we were watching that Fat Bastard we saw how careful she is" Geoff said.

"Well the way I see it is her security will work for us and against us, against us because it is so tight, but for us because it is, so tight" The dummy said looking at him with staring eyes.

"That doesn't make sense" Geoff said sipping his tea again.

"Yes it does, if we can get into her place, then the security will keep everyone else out, she lives alone we have deduced that from when we watched her before remember"

"Yes as far as we could see she lives there alone but it is tight and secure, there is no way we can get in, who do you think we are bloody cat burglars"

"You disappoint me sometimes, we use magic, we use skill and we use brains"

"Magic, you mean tricks, it will not be as easy as last time, placing a card in a wallet while he is busy or using a trick deck" Geoff shook his head.

"Magic which is our magic, ok, my magic all you need to do is get me in there, and I can do the rest, I can get you in and we then have all the night to play" the mouth opened into a wide hideous grin and the whole dummy shook and laughed a malevolent laugh.

"You enjoy this too much you know that" Geoff said looking over at the insane smile on the dummies face looking back at him.

"It is all I have" the dummy said without moving its lips.

"Yeah, ok well let's think about how this is going to work"

"Oh I have already I have all bloody day and night to think about it, I have a few ideas we just need to get in there, you need to practice your telekinesis"

"I can't do it like you, never have been able to, I try but nothing moves, you are the one with that skill" Geoff said drinking his tea

"It is power not skill, a skill can be learned but power commands" the head turned from side to side and the mouth snapped shut in a fast action that caused a clap sound.

"Well there you go, I do not have the power like you" Geoff looked at the dummy and saw the eye brows lift then drop and the mouth chatter, and the head turned to look at him.

"I hope you are not mocking me sir, the dummy said in a slow different voice"

"Would I ever do that, do that to you?" Geoff said in the same slow voice.

The dummy rocked back and laughed out loud, shaking as it did on the settee. Then calmed down and turned its head slowly looking at Geoff but not speaking.

Geoff leaned back and drank his tea, when he had finished it he stood up and washed out the cup drying it and putting it away in the cupboard. When he came back into the room the dummy was gone from the settee. Geoff paid it no more attention and sat down on the settee and watched a little bit of TV before he went to bed. There in the bed room was the dummy sat in the corner, its head tilted to one side eyes shut and the whole body limp. It looked like it had just been thrown there and left. Ignoring it Geoff brushed his teeth and got into bed, it was Friday tomorrow and at least he would have two days off from that bloody place he worked and the power trip, big I am, bitch that had been put in charge, he sighed out and thought about his options, he knew he had been there to long and it should be time to move on, it should be time for a lot of things in his life he thought, then settled in to sleep.

CHAPTER THREE

"Leaving work the next day he walked alone out of the factory, everyone else talking and chatting about meeting up that night for a drink or a football match the next day. But he never got asked, not anymore, because he never went and never really wanted too. He kept himself to himself and most people left him alone which was the way he liked it really. He was never a people person even when he was young. It had carried over into his adult life and he had no problem with it. He got into his car and steadily drove towards the shops and home but took a detour first. It was too a new housing estate that had been there only a few years, posh and up market the houses ridiculously priced and not really that well built. Modern buildings are nowhere near as good as the old ones, he and his dad had spoke about it many times which is one reason his parents would never move they liked the solid brick built house they were in and knew the history of it and were the only ones to ever live in it. He drove slowly down the street and then turned left. He got a few looks from people in their gardens, they had not seen this car here before and it was a Ford, no one on here had a Ford, it was BMW or Jaguar at least. He paid them no attention and slowly drove down and stopped at the bottom of the road. He was looking at a large detached house. Electric gates at the front and completely walled off all round the perimeter. There were cameras placed on top of two stone pillars by the gate and several more across the outer wall, then some more on the entrance to the house it's self. The lawn was large and well cut the whole exterior was clean and tidy. She obviously hired a gardener to do all this work for her. A large white SUV with a private number plate was parked in the long drive outside the front door. He sighed and shook his head he knew he had no chance of getting in there.

Turning round he drove home and thought about how it could be done, but he was hindered by the fact he was not one hundred percent certain he wanted to anymore. The main objective was to revenge his sister and that had been done and was over and they had got away with it. Yes there were more like him and they were vile people but, were it really down to him to do anything about it? He knew Dummy wanted it, he knew he was looking forward to it. And he knew what the dummy wanted the dummy more than often got. He closed his eyes and remembered something. Something in his childhood that had haunted him ever since. He shook his head and discarded it from his mind. He went shopping to buy his weekly food shop, going in and out as fast as he could he didn't like crowded places. Then headed home and was happy he had two days away from that bloody place he worked. Parking up in his designated place, he took the two bags from the back and went into the apartment block. Going up the one flight of stairs he let himself into his place and shut the door behind him.

He saw the dummy stood by the window looking out across the small field and beyond up the hillside that lead into the neighboring estate. He paid it no attention and went to the kitchen to put away his food supplies. When he came back out to the main room the dummy was sat in its chair. It turned its head and looked at him, watching him walk across the room and sit on the settee. It didn't move its head just its eyes, then snapped its head round to face him when he sat down.

"You are later than normal, have you been somewhere?" It said to him

"I went to have another look where she lives and around the place. It is very well secured and there are cameras all over the bloody place, the neighborhood is close knit and I stood out like a bloody sore thumb." Geoff told it looking across as it stared at him.

"And? We knew all this from before we said it would be hard to get to her, but we said we would find a way" the eyes blinked once and the mouth dropped open.

"I know what we said, I am just saying the house looks a no go area that is all"

"You are losing your nerve, just like you always did; you are going back on it"

"I am not going back on anything, I am being practical, playing it safe" Geoff told it with a raised voice.

"Playing it safe? Ha, that is a laugh do you know what date it is today, have you any idea what date it is today Geoffrey?" The dummy said with wide eyes and tilted head.

"I am aware what day it is, you remind me every fucking year what this date is, thank you very much" He stood up and went into the Kitchen area and made himself some tea and got some chocolate biscuits he had bought then came back into the front room. The Dummy was looking at him and moved its head still staring has he walked past and went to sit down. It said nothing but stared at him its wooden features blank and cold and heartless. Its eyes staring out of the sockets not blinking just a blank lifeless stare, finally it spoke.

"Twenty years now, twenty years, do you realize how long twenty years is?" its voice was cold and emotionless. Geoff closed his eyes he was going to have his afternoon nap. He drifted off into a troubled sleep and remembered and revisited his youth.

****

Brothers could be close, but these two were very close they were twins after all; they went and did everything together. Geoff and his slightly younger brother by ten minutes, Danny, playing in the back garden of their parent's house. Danny acted as if he was

41

the greatest magician that ever lived and always came up with tricks to and elusions to perform. Maybe no one ever saw them, except their mum and dad, but to them it was real magic. Danny wore this black cape and was very extravagant when he was pretending to do magic. Geoff took it more as a bit of fun, but lately Danny had become more and more serious. He wanted to try a trick for real he wanted to do some real magic.

"Black Magic Geoff that is where the real power is, Black Magic"

"There is no such thing you dummy" Geoff said laughing.

"Do not laugh, I have something and we can try something, I am sure we can make it work" his voice had become low and secretive.

"What is it then, some magic potion?" Geoff asked getting a little intrigued.

"Nope but soon we will go out when it is late and we will try it out, you better not tell mum or I will kill you, this is top secret and between you and me and only you and me. Do you understand?" Danny took Geoff by the throat and held him there looking into his eyes for an answer, Geoff nodded and pulled away as the pain was getting worse as Danny tightened his grip and then laughed out loud.

They carried on playing in the garden until their dad came home. Then they were shouted in told to wash up and they sat down for dinner. Sitting at the dinner table they all began to eat. Dad at the head of the table and mum sat across from him, the two boys on either side.

"So what have you two been up too" dad said with a full mouth of food he chewed as he looked at them both in turn.

"Doing magic dad, we are magicians" Danny told him with enthusiasm

"That is good I hope you can make all the washing up disappear later give your mother a rest, while it is school holidays you are going to be helping out around the house"

"Yes dad" Geoff said

"Whatever you say father" Danny said rather sarcastically, and sighed out and huffed in despair almost at the thought of it.

"It is what I say and don't you bloody forget it son, I am not going to work all day and your mother seeing to the house all day just for you to pratt about in the Garden, I want chores done while you are off school is that clear?" he took a big mouthful of food and chewed it looking at Danny for an answer.

"Yes" was all he got has he continued to eat his food. After dinner the two boys did the washing up and dad went into this shed.

Mum was sat in the living room and smiled at them both as they came back in

"Thank you kind sir's that is a big help" she said still smiling at them.

Danny went to the sideboard and brought back a deck of cards, he went to his mum and told her to pick a card, she smiled and did so, and she held it in her hand.

"OK, show it to Geoff" Danny said.

"Nope, he will tell you what it is" she smirked then laughed.

"Ok, don't then, now put it back in the deck" he held out the deck of cards in his hand and closed his eyes. She looked at him and made sure he didn't peek, she placed the card in the middle of the deck. He opened his eyes and gave her the deck.

"Right what now?" she asked

"Shuffle the deck mum" Danny told her then after she had done he took the cards from her. He fanned them out into his hand then back again and then looked at his mother.

"Concentrate on your card mum" Geoff said.

"I am doing" she told them both. Danny looked at her intently and then fingered through the deck of cards, placing some into his other hand he went about three quarters the way through. Then gave his mother a card face down, she held it in her hand and looked at him.

"Ok mum what was your card?" Danny asked.

"It was the jack of diamonds" she said

"Look" he said staring down at the car in her hand; she turned it over and was astonished that is was the jack of diamonds.

"Oh My God how did you do that?" she gasped

"Magic" is all he said then looking at Geoff he ran off up stairs, Geoff followed and mum was left looking at the deck of cards and trying to figure out how he did the trick.

Both boys shared a room and it was full of magic things like props and magic memorabilia. Walls were covered with posters of magic symbols and pictures of magicians. The side table had magic trick props on it and Geoff had a box in the corner and it was something he had been bought that Christmas. He was trying to become a Ventriloquist but was not very good at it. The box had remained unopened for weeks. Danny sat on the bed and smiled

"Did you see mums face" he laughed out loud and was proud he had do the trick well.

"Yeah you have got that trick down to a tee now little brother"

"Well I have more ideas and when we try something soon it will be amazing" his eye lit up when he said it and a smile came across his face.

"What do you mean, what are you trying?" Geoff asked curious then going to lie down on his single bed across from his brother. He clasped his hands behind his head and lay on his back and looked up at the ceiling.

"Black Magic, it is the strongest magic there is" He laid out on his bed too as the boys talked to each other.

"No, that can be dangerous, you have to be careful I know someone who did a séance and they invited a demon into their house and now can't get shut of it"

"That may be so but if you can master the black arts, your magic is the best"

"You have to be careful, it can be very dangerous" Geoff said with a frown.

"Stop being a wimp, you never want to try anything, live for once" he shook his head and turned to look over at his brother.

"I want to learn how to move things by looking at them, control people's minds, make them do whatever I want them too" there was an excitement in his voice. His eyes were wide when he was talking and he was genuinely thrilled about the prospect.

"Yeah, make all the girls like you and want you, make rich people give you their money" Geoff said turning to face his twin brother.

"Make the people you don't like jump off a bridge" Danny laughed at the thought of it.

"Don't be stupid you dummy that's murder"

"No because I will never get caught I will be controlling their minds and be nowhere near them, I will never get caught" he said with enjoyment in his voice at the thought of it.

"I don't know I just want lots of money and lots of girls" Geoff was content with what he said and smiled at the thought of it too.

"Well I have done a bit of reading up on it on the internet and there is a way, we need to go out one night you and me, with something I have"

"What is it, how can we get out on a night we are not allowed"

"Stop being soft, we will sneak out and it will be amazing you will see"

"If you say so little brother if you say so" Geoff turned back and yawned.

"It is going to be amazing you will see and tell no one, or else" Danny said firmly.

"Geoff, Geoff" the dummy shouted and woke him with shock of surprise.

"What is it" he said looking round and waking up quickly.

"You are snoring, it is driving me mad" The dummy snarled at him

Geoff sat up and yawned out, then stood up and walked into the kitchen he was hungry and wanted some food. The dummy shouted from the living area.

"We have to plan, I want to get to it right away, and we need to get to the bitch"

"Well right now I am making myself some food so it will have to wait" Geoff shouted back and began to make himself dinner. He had head ache and went to get some tablets from the bathroom cabinet, he didn't look at the dummy when he left the room but did on his return.

"You are getting a lot of headaches again" the dummy told him staring at him has he walked past and into the kitchen area again.

"I will live, I have done until now"

"You are getting them more and more; it is not healthy to get so many headaches"

"Like I said I will live" Geoff walked up to the little table and begun to set it out with knife and fork and a drink.

"Why you sitting up there again, you use to sit with your food on your knee here, on the settee, what is wrong with you lately" The dummy spun its head round with a jerk and its mouth dropped open.

"I like sitting at the table, its more civilized" Geoff said going back into the kitchen area.

"It is also away from me, I might get the idea you are trying to avoid me, I might get the idea you don't like me anymore" the dummy's voice was slower and deeper.

"Why would you do that that would be really stupid" Geoff said from the kitchen area but didn't come round to look at the dummy as he spoke.

"Do you remember what we did to that fat ugly disgusting agent, do you remember his eyes bulging from his head, the white stuff coming from his mouth, the tongue swelling as the rope tightened round his neck, it was wonderful to see" the macabre laugh was chilling that the dummy did and it rocked its head as it laughed out loud.

Geoff closed his eyes and shook his head, he said nothing and just made his food, it didn't take too long and he sat and ate it in silence at the table. He could hear the dummy humming and quietly chatting to its self. He didn't say anything to it he just finished his food and then went and washed the dishes up, dried them and put them away he cleaned the kitchen and came back into the room. He sat on the settee and looked over at the dummy looking at him humming to its self. He looked away and said nothing.

"Is your head ache gone now?" the dummy asked him

"Yes for the most part it has" Geoff answered not looking at it.

"I hope you are not going to go quiet like you use too, because that pisses me off, do you hear me,?" the dummy shouted at him.

"Yes I bloody hear you I never stop hearing you. I hear your voice at work all the time in my head you are never away from me" Geoff snapped back at it.

"Well that is good I am please about that, because we are a team you and me, we can never be apart you know that don't you" The dummy lifted its eye brows and bared its teeth in a hideous smile.

"How could I forget, you have been there all the time, I have no life because of it"

"I hope that was not resentment I hope that was not hostility" the dummy said to him

"I have no girlfriend because of you, we live here because of you, you run my bloody life, why the hell do you think I get headaches all the time, stress bloody stress"

"Oh please do get a girlfriend, bring her back here, let me watch" The dummy winked one eye and grinned again.

"You are not funny, just leave me alone tonight I want some quiet time" Geoff shot a stare at the dummy staring at him. It closed its eyes and didn't make another sound all evening. Geoff watched a film then went to bed. He left the dummy in its chair in the living area when he turned in and soon was falling asleep and dreaming again.

****

"Ok listen Danny said, I am going to will that cup there to move, I am going to use the power of my mind to move that object" Geoff had put the cup on the side of the sink they both stared at it and Danny concentrated. He put his two fingers to his temple and was staring intensely at the cup. Geoff was stood next to him.

"What the bloody hell are you doing" Their dad's voice thundered out at them from the doorway. It made both of them jump and they turned round.

"Making that cup move just using my mind" Danny told him.

"No, you use your hands and while you are at it do the bloody washing up, come on I want it done now" he said and walked back out of the kitchen. Geoff jumped to it and started to wash up the dishes. Danny just cursed and put two fingers up at where his dad had been stood.

"Come on let's get it done" Geoff told him has he started to wash the dirty dishes and Danny reluctantly helped him.

When they had finished they both came back into the living room where their mother and father were watching some TV. Both boys sat down on the couch and said nothing. They knew not to disturb their father if he was watching the Television. The program did not interest them at all and Danny nudged his brother and they both went off up to their room.

Closing the door behind them Danny became very secretive and went to his bed, he pulled a small suitcase from under it and took something out. Then went and listened at the door again. Coming back he put the board on his bed and had something in his hand. Geoff came over and had a look at it. He had not seen anything like it before.

"What is it, what does it do?" Geoff asked

"This big brother is a magic board, a witch board" Danny proudly announced

"A what, what does it do,, what is that in your hand?" he pointed to the thing Danny was holding.

"This is the pointer, you put it on the board and you can talk with the dead and also get great powers from spirits, I have read up about it on the internet" Danny said excited

"Hold on, no, them things are dangerous" he backed away and shook his head

"Stop being soft, this is our way to becoming the greatest Magicians the world has ever seen, you can try your hypnosis and I can do move things with my mind we will be a great magic act. World famous and make lots of money, you will see" He was smiled from ear to ear has he looked down at the board on his bed. It had numbers zero to nine printed on it and also every letter of the alphabet. A yes and a no. he put the wooded pointer on the board and looked over to Geoff. Who was stood by the door not sure what to do, he could see his brother was very excited but he was worried and didn't know what to do or say. He was not sure of this and it scared him somewhat.

"Where did you get it from?" Geoff asked.

"I get it from the internet, bought it with my Christmas money I had left over, went to pick it up yesterday and had to hide it under my bed. They were not going to sell it to me at first but I told them it was for my dad and would come back with proof later"

"You are going to get into trouble Danny, what happens when they find out?"

"They won't I gave a false address and name, paid cash that was all they were bothered about as soon as they saw the money they gave me the board and ran"

"What do you mean ran?"

"We met in the park, by the old band stand no one could see us there" Danny looked at him then back to his board.

"That is all very strange don't you think, very weird"

"Oh shut up Geoff, come on let's give it a try, put something by the door so they can't get in straight away, and listen out for anyone coming up the stairs"

He put the pointer on the board and put his fingers onto it, then looked at Geoff who came over and watched. The pointer dashed over the board and Geoff pounced backwards in fright. Danny fell about laughing and pointed at him calling him stupid because it was him doing it.

"Stop messing around with it, could be very dangerous you dummy" Geoff protested

"Shut up, you have no balls, right let's try it" Danny put the pointer on the board again and placed his finger tips onto it. He breathed in and spoke softly

"Is there anyone there, give me a sign, point to a letter, speak to me" he said and waited. He looked at Geoff who was looking at the board. Nothing happened and Danny tried again.

Nothing happened and he was becoming agitated. He repeated his words but with more vigor and much more commanding, but again nothing happened.

"You come put your fingers on it too" he told Geoff.

"No, I dare not" Geoff said backing off.

"Do it now you, or I will smash your face in" Danny snarled at him violently, Geoff reluctantly came over and placed his fingers on the pointer as well.

"Speak to us, show us you are there show us the magic we seek" Danny said forcefully

But still nothing happened, it was silent and it was still. Danny threw the pointer across the board and backed off annoyed. Geoff backed off too he just stared at the board while Danny stood his arms folded and he was in a huff.

They put the board away in the suitcase under Danny's bed and said no more about it. They went down stairs and got a glass of water. They noticed their father hitting the TV, the signal had drifted out or something he said. They paid it no notice and went to bed. Unknown to Geoff at the time Danny had tried again that night by himself and he did most nights when everyone was asleep. Then one night on the full moon, he tried and he felt something. It was like a shiver going through his body. It emanated from the wooden pointer he had in his hands. He was not sure but he thought he felt it move and shake. He was excited and scared at the same time. He was going to wake Geoff but decided not to. He put the board away and went to sleep he had a nightmare that night and woke everyone up shouting in his sleep. He felt silly and embarrass about it. His father called him a stupid silly lad and wanted him to settle back down. His mother gave him comfort and Geoff asked if he was alright. He didn't like the fuss and pushed them away. He fell asleep again and was never the same again after that night and it was when things started to change.

CHAPTER FOUR

Geoff woke up the next morning, his head ache gone he had slept late and felt better for it. He looked over and saw the dummy at the bottom of his bed looking at him. He paid it no attention and rolled over stretching out.

"Today is Saturday, I think we need to go and start making some plans" the dummy said to him. Has he turned back around and sat up in bed.

"I have told you the place is not possible to break into, we can't follow her and kidnap her can we, this is not the movies this is not fantasy it is real life" Geoff said then yawned and stretched his arms out wide as he did.

"This is what it is, and all you have to do is get me in there, I can do the rest and you will just be able to walk right in I will let you in" the dummy was talking to him straight and getting a little agitated as it did at Geoff's lack of enthusiasm.

"You are getting carried away with it and it is not as easy as that" Geoff insisted

"No, it is not that, not that at all, it is you, you have lost your nerve lost your gusto you just don't want to do it anymore" The dummy opened its mouth wide then snapped it shut and the eyes opened and shut uncontrollably.

"It is not that, we said she deserve what she gets yes, we said she is just as guilty as anyone yes, but the reality of it is we just got away with Murder, and I am now thinking we should leave it, we need to be safe and careful" Geoff got out of bed quickly and sighed out loud as he did. The dummy spun its head round and looked at him go past its eyes wide and staring at him. Geoff went into the toilet then returned a little time later. The dummy was sat on the pillow now and looking at him the blank stare and cold look it had.

Geoff started to get dressed; he ignored the dummy staring at him and left the room. He went towards the kitchen area and made himself some tea. He came back into the living room and the dummy was sat in its chair looking at him. He sat down on the settee and turned to stare back at the dummy holding his tea in his hand.

They looked at each other for a long minute then Geoff turned away and took a drink of his hot tea; he put the mug down and leaned back on the settee saying in a calm voice.

"Do you not see what I am saying; if we get caught I go to prison you end up on the scrap heap, or burnt or something worse" we have to be careful.

"Careful yes, but not blind and forgiving no" The dummy said in a calm voice back to him.

"Forgiving, what do you mean we know of her dealings with children in the sex trade, or we think we do, but she has done nothing to us personally, we are not bloody crusaders?"

"What if the fat agent Bastard had given Cynthia to her when he had finished, what if you found out she had her, and was selling her to the sick bastards to come and abuse her, got her dependant on drugs and trapped in a vicious circle of pain and torture" the dummy was still and no movement was made from it at all it was just blank and still.

"You are spouting a lot of what if's there, obviously if she had Cynthia then it would be different but she has not and never will have, she is safe and always will be"

"You don't know that, she will never be the same again, you said so yourself"

"Yes I did, but murdering this woman will not help her will it" Geoff took a drink of his tea.

"It will help others and she will get what she deserves, I want to get it done, and you will help me to do it, look how good we were the last time, you were all for that and I think you really enjoyed it to be honest I could tell" the dummy said expressionless

"No, you enjoyed it I did not, I did that for Cynthia, and that is why we did it. I played a part there and it served a purpose, it imbedded fear into him which was the idea"

"Rubbish, absolute Bollocks, you enjoyed it you planned it you were all for it, and you were for these others too, but now you have lost your nerve, second thoughts. Pathetic you always have been the weak one, the one who backed off and was scared"

"No, I was being cautious and careful, you just want to barge in and you like the suffering you cause, like I said it is me who would go to prison not you"

"Aw are we scared, are we wetting our pants, you need to get some balls. You need to wake up to reality you need to fucking start listening to me" The dummy blinked its eyes and the head spun around a full one hundred and eighty degrees, coming to a sudden stop and staring at him. Geoff slowly turned and looked down at the dummy he said nothing and just drank his tea in silence. He leaned back and his thoughts drifted back.

****

Danny had gone quieter lately, Geoff noticed it and so did his mother; they came home from playing outside and were sat at the dinner table. They were eating their food and no one saying anything. Then Danny started to giggle to himself. Geoff looked at him and saw he was looking over to his father, who had just used the salt pot and put it back down on the table. Paying no more attention to it he looked away then jumped, and made everyone else jump as he pushed back on his chair cursing.

"What is it, love?" Their mother said.

"The bloody salt pot just flew off the table"

"You knocked it you mean, thinks do not just fly off the table by themselves dear" she said shaking her head.

"I never touched the bloody thing I am telling you" he complained wiping the salt off his legs and picking the salt pot up off the floor. Danny was trying not to laugh; he hid it while he ate. Geoff noticed it though, and was going to make sure he asked him about it later.

The rest of the meal went without incident; Danny was staring at the TV for a short while then headed off up stairs. Geoff helped his mother to do the dishes and their father sat in his chair and turned on the Television set. He cursed and started to bang the remote control in his hand then get up and do the same with the Television.

"He is going to smash that damn thing one of these days" his mum said to Geoff as they cleaned away in the kitchen.

"What is wrong with it?" Geoff asked looking round the door to where his dad was stood over the television banging it with his hand.

"I don't know he keeps hitting the bloody thing, knocked something lose I imagine"

"It was alright last night when we watched it?" Geoff said coming back up to his mother and taking a plate from her to dry with the towel.

"I know love, looks like we are going to have to get another one soon though don't you think" she said with a rolling of her eyes as she heard the banging noise and cursing coming from the front room.

"Probably yes" Geoff agreed with a smile and they both started to laugh as the swearing got louder from the front room and the banging more rapid.

"What's wrong with this bloody thing, its bloody useless piece of shit" he said hitting it again

Geoff came up to his room a little later Danny was laid on the bed he was just looking up at the ceiling. He said nothing when Geoff lay onto his own bed and turning onto his side propping his head up on his arm asked.

"So what is wrong with you?"

"Did you see him jump tonight, funny wasn't it" Danny said not moving.

"He dropped the salt shaker"

"Did he?" Danny smiled and giggled

"What are you laughing at?"

"Nothing"

"Dad pissed off the TV won't work" Geoff informed him

"I know" again Danny giggled

"I do not know why you keep giggling what are you laughing at?"

"You will see, everyone will see and you will know and be jealous"

"You are being stupid and annoying you have changed, why are you so quiet these days what is wrong?" Geoff asked then lay on his back looking up his hands clasped behind his head.

"Nothing is wrong now, there was a lot wrong but now nothing is wrong"

"You are going mad, stupid and insane" Geoff said closing his eyes and taking a nap after his meal. Danny turned his head and looked over at his brother, then smiled and turned back. He giggled and put his hand over his mouth as he did.

"Maybe but I don't need your help anymore we don't need to go out anywhere anymore I can do it all here by myself, you will see" Danny said and turned away.

"Yeah whatever"   Geoff answered he was only half listening anyway.

It was late that night it was still it was quiet, Geoff who normally was a heavy sleeper. Woke up and happened to look over to Danny's bed, he could just see has his eyes were becoming adjusted to the dark that the bed was empty. He sat up and Saw Danny was sat in the corner his back towards him. The way he was sat and positioned it was perfect for the strong moon light to come through and illuminate him. He was looking at something down on the floor his hands in front of him. Geoff got up onto his knees and tried to see what he was doing. He could hear Danny whispering and moving something in front of him but he didn't know what.

He watched for a little while then lay back down and watched him from a laid down position and if he turned around he could simply shut his eyes and Danny wouldn't know he had seen him. A fear grew inside him as he got a glimpse of what he was doing; he caught sight of the witch board on the floor. Danny was using it and softly talking to it. Geoff silently gasped and a shiver went through his body. He wanted to get up and confront his brother but something told him not too, a fear had rose inside him and this was something he had never felt before and it scared him, it scared him to death. He could feel himself shaking and he closed his eyes when Danny seem to finish, he heard him putting the board away under the bed and then getting back into bed. He thought he heard a laugh and then it was silent. He was shaking and dare not open his eyes. He didn't get any sleep that night. He was afraid to go to sleep; he slowly and slightly opened his eyes from time to time. But Danny never moved and seemed fast as sleep. His throat was dry and he tried to swallow. He didn't know what to do and was confused by it. Why was he afraid to confront his little brother? They had always been close. But something in his guts told him something was not right.

The next day Danny seemed fine but Geoff was quiet, he tried but could not hide his difference and his brother noticed it very soon. It was after school walking home when Danny mentioned something.

"There is something wrong with you, and I think I know what it is, it is fear" Danny said as they walked home along the pavement.

"I am fine, what is wrong with you?" Geoff asked.

"Come with me" Danny said pulling his arm and heading off down the embankment and across the field into the wooded area behind their house. They sometimes headed this way home in the summer. Danny was gripping Geoff's arm tight and pulling him along they went into the wooded area and off along the path into the trees. Geoff fought but Danny's grip was tight. They eventually got into a scuffle and Geoff threw him off Danny pushing him away.

"Get off, what the hell you doing, Dummy" Geoff shouted at him.

Danny stood in front of him and smiled, he then laughed and his head rocked back has he did.

"He sounded insane almost and it scared Geoff to the fact he stepped back a few paces.

"You have no idea, I was going to share it with you but you are not strong enough, I know that now, but let me tell you this Brother, I am on my way and I have the power flowing through me" Danny smiled and looked Geoff directly in the eye.

"You are bloody mad, what the hell is wrong with you?" Geoff backed up a few more paces.

"I have found it, found how to become magic" he grinned and put his arms out in front of him and looked up into the sky.

"Found what, what have you found?" Geoff was becoming concerned and didn't like or notice Danny anymore in this state of mind at all.

"The power of darkness" he laughed.

"Shut up you dummy you are just being stupid" Geoff nervously laughed at him.

Looking at Geoff Danny smiled then he looked around and picked up a small branch that had fallen from a nearby tree. He threw it in front of Geoff's feet. Geoff looked down at it then at Danny. Who looked at the branch and concentrated. Geoff thought he saw the little branch move slightly then it stood up on its end by its self and lifted a few inches off the ground before falling back down. Danny was smiling big across his face and looked at Geoff, who was staring at the branch with his mouth open.

"Pick it up you will see it is just a normal bit of wood, I can do it with just about anything, like salt shakers" he laughed out loud remembering his dad getting covered in salt at the table and also banging the "broken" TV set.

Geoff slowly picked up the branch and could see it was just as he said a piece of wood. He threw it away and looked over in amazement at his Brother.

"How, how did you do that?" he said shaking but still excited somewhat.

"I told you, I have found magic" Danny sighed and smiled. He walked over to his brother and put his arm round his shoulder.

"Found it where? What sort of magic?" Geoff asked him with a shaky voice

"Don't be afraid, I am in control and will get much stronger, you could come too if you wanted too, but you must, must never tell anyone is that clear"

"Yes but how?" Geoff looked over to where he had thrown the branch.

"You need to understand this is top secret, no one must ever know, you must promise me this right here and right now, and if the secret is broken you will go straight to hell"

"I promise, but is this safe what is it you have to do?"

"Sell your soul to the Devil" Danny said seriously but then burst out laughing seeing the shock on his brother's face.

"Shut up you bloody dummy" Geoff said as they started to walk back home. Strangely Geoff felt a little more at ease. Maybe because Danny was more responsive and welcoming, whatever the reason both their lives were to change forever.

****

Taking his empty mug back to the sink he washed it out and put it away. He came back down onto the settee and looked at the dummy staring at him from the chair.

"You enjoy it too much and it is going to get us caught, but if you want me to get you in there it might work, especially if you hide when they find her and then sneak out at a later time, when it is empty or something" Geoff said to the dummy looking at him.

"This is what we agreed before, but I want you there with me, I will do what is needed but I want you involved and need you to do something's" The dummy said monosyllabically.

"What things, you said you wanted to do something yourself, on your own, just needed my help to get you into the place?"

"No, that was one option, but I want to make her suffer, do you realise the suffering she as caused young girls, do you know the money she has made from it, I am tired of you changing your mind every fucking day, one minute you are all for it then you change your mind, you are just chicken, always have been" the mouth dropped open and the eyes blinked as the head turned to the side and then back.

"I am cautious" Geoff defended

"Bollocks it is called chicken shit, spineless, no balls, scared"

"It is none of them it is just I am not as fucking insane as you" Geoff raised his voice slightly

"Insane, fucking insane, do you realise have you any idea, you will never know, you will never understand the torment, you will never know so do not piss me off or you will know what will happen." The voice of the dummy became menacing and lower in tone.

Geoff turned away and sighed out, he stood up and walked to the window he looked out over the field behind his apartment block and then up beyond onto the field. He was alone with his thoughts for a moment then turned round. The dummy was now sat on the floor looking up at him. Its head tilted to one side.

"I will do you a deal, we will go for this bitch and then that is it, no more, none of the others we think are involved, we forget it and that is the end of it" Geoff said looking down at the dummy on the floor, who slowly tilted its head to look up at him.

"Deal" it said slowly and quietly. Geoff reached down and picked it up and walked into the bed room he threw the dummy on the bed like he was discarding a piece of rubbish. He left it there where it fell all sprawled out on its belly. He took a shower and got a shave. He dressed and got ready. The dummy was sat in the corner now looking at him.

"What is the plan of action?" it said dropping its mouth open on the last word.

"We need some sort of plan; I do not want to keep going round to her house, because my car has been seen there already. Do you remember when we were watching before and she kept visiting that fat agent Bastard. We saw her visit him a few times"

"Yes, I remember" The dummy said not really following.

"Well the secretary must have seen her come and go, lots of times more than we did"

"So she will know things we don't?" the dummy lifted its eye brows as it spoke.

"I think she is much more involved then she lets on, she was obviously fucking him and must have known what they were up too"

"Let's torture the bitch and find out, I like it" the dummy said excited and the whole wooded body shook and its head rocked from side to side.

"No, let's see if we can hypnotiser her, she was very vulnerable and pretty easy to control I think I can do it again." Geoff said shaking his head

"Oh, you want to try that, ok but if it doesn't work I want it done my way"

"You are just a sick little wooded Dummy you know that?"

"I sure do folks, and for my next trick" it said spinning its head completely around and opening its eyes it suddenly rose off the ground and stood up on its own two legs.

"Wow you will be tying your own shoe laces soon" Geoff said sarcastically

The room door slammed shut, and the dummy looked at him then the door, and back to him again, Geoff was not impressed and walked out of the room opening the door as he did and giving an uninterested look back at the dummy.

A short time later they were driving down the road where the Agents office was, they drove past slowly and noticed it was still open. Geoff parked up down the road a way and got out. He locked the door and left the dummy in a case on the back seat.

He looked around as he walked down towards the office, he didn't really like coming back here but he knew it was the place to start from. The office block was used by several different companies so he hoped he was going to get lucky and she was still here. He walked up the few stone steps and went in through the two brown wooded doors.

It was all just has he remembered it from before but the one office he wanted to go too was closed and the name of the agent was no longer on the door. He cursed under his breath and looked round at the old man security guard looking at him from the doorway. He had not noticed him when he had come in, and a sudden sinking feeling hit his stomach. If he had not seen him just now had he not seen him the last time?

"Can I help you sir" the old man said looking straight at him but with old weary eyes.

"Oh sorry didn't see you there, have you worked here long?" Geoff asked.

"Nope, just started, there was an incident and they decided to put some security in place"

"Oh I see" Geoff said relived and he walked over to where the man was.

"I have been away and just come back, but seem to remember someone mentioning there is an agent here, or some kind of talent scout" Geoff shook his head pretending to be confused.

"Nope, he is gone, not there anymore, what do you want with him?" the old man sat down slowly and carefully on a chair which was just inside the door way but off to the left, which is why Geoff didn't notice him there in the first place.

"Just someone mentioned him is all, I want to be a singer and looking for an agent you know" Geoff said regrettable and wished he had put it better.

"Well no one here to help you, only two offices occupied now and none of them are agents"

"Oh I am wasting my time then, I don't suppose you know where he went or is there a number he left, maybe with his secutary or something" Geoff enquired.

"Nope, there was a young little thing here a few times but she had not been back for over a week now, cleared the office out she did" the old man sighed out and leaned back in his chair. The uniform he had on was too big for him and he must be well over retirement age. Geoff thought they had just done it for show, they can now say they have security in the building and all is safe. They will pay him next to nothing and that is all he as to do. Security in name only and filled the requirement of the statement, "we have security".

Geoff looked around and could see there was no cameras, he looked around a second time and then came close to the old man, he knelt down in front of him. He looked into the old man's eyes and he looked back a little confused.

"Just want you to listen to my voice, it is all you need to hear, I want you to listen and look into my eyes" Geoff said softly and in a soothing voice.

"What, what you talking about" the old man said shaking his head. Geoff held up his index finger on his right hand and moved it from side to side in a rhythmic fashion. The old man looked at it and Geoff spoke again.

"Just listen to my voice, it is all you need to hear, take deep breaths for me, relax and breathe. Look at my finger and listen to my voice"

The old man at first looked confused and scared but eventually he relaxed into a calm state, his eyes were getting heavy and he concentrated on the finger and Geoff's soothing voice. It didn't take long and seemed easier then Geoff had hoped, he just kept the calm and ease going then he noticed the old ma started to drop into a trance like state. Geoff knew this was a signal that he was becoming responsive to Geoff's suggestions. His breathing slowed and he became still, motionless and with a blank look on his face.

"Just listen to my voice; it is all you need to hear do you understand?"

"Yes" the old man said slowly

"Good, when I clap my hands you will wake up and remember nothing, do you understand?"

"Yes" the old man said calmly and obediently

"Good, there was a young girl who worked here, do you remember her, you saw her"

"Yes" the old man said blankly

"Is she still here?" Geoff asked

"No, she is not"

Geoff cursed, and then looked round again. He was still moving his finger and the old man was still transfixed on it.

"Do you know where she works now?"

"Yes"

"Can you tell me the address?"

"Book, it is in the book"

"Where, what book, can you get me it?"

The old man stood up looking bemused and dazed, he went into a very small office off to the side, came out with an address book opened it and showed Geoff the address. Geoff memorised it and told him to put the book back. He sat the old man down and walked to the door. He stepped outside and turned clapping his hands as he closed the door quietly. He was gone and the old man woke out of his trance and looked round he remembered nothing and just sat there looking forward.

Geoff hurried back to his car; he got in and heard the muffled voice from inside the case on the back seat. He leaned back and opened it. The dummy was laid flat on its back looking up.

"Well is she there, did you see her, what happened?" it asked not moving from its position.

"She doesn't work there anymore the office is all closed, but I have an address where she is now, and it is not too far away"

"Well what the hell you waiting for lets go, time is a wasting" The dummy shouted

"I had to put an old gentleman under for the information"

"Lovely well done, top of the class for easy hypnosis, now let us get going and find this bitch, then onto the other bigger bitch" the dummy's voice sounded excited and eager to get on with it, It didn't sit well with Geoff and he looked back at it with distaste.

"We will go and see if it is possible" Geoff said

"Yeah, yeah let's get going"

Geoff started the car and pulled off slowly and headed down the road, he drove carefully and went to the address the old man had given him. He looked down the road and saw the office block were the address had taken him too. It seemed much busier and more secure. He drove in and parked up into the visitor's car park. He looked round and could see it was again a multi office complex so she could be anywhere in there. But then he noticed something in the near car park. It was a large SUV. The same one he had seen the day before outside the house. It was hers the woman they were after.

"What does it look like, let me see" The dummy said from the back.

"Well, well, isn't it a small world" Geoff said lifting the dummy back up and into the front seat so it could see round.

"What, what is it?" the dummy said moving its eyes from side to side.

"That white SUV, look at the number plate" Geoff said has they looked at each.

"Well cut me off at the knees and call me tripod" the dummy said dropping its jaw open.

"She must of poached her here, too much of a coincidence I think wouldn't you say?"

"Yep, something definitely going on, it must be a front a cover or something"

"Well it makes our job a bit easier, already answered the questions if she knows her and is still in touch with her"

"Oh yes, and now the game is going to move up a notch, we need to find out where she works in there, we need to find out what she does"

"Cameras everywhere we will have to wait until she leaves, then follow then see where she takes us" Geoff drove off slowly and out of the car park. He made a note of the place and where he was so when he returns he will know where he is.

"Do you think slutty secretary will be in there now, with the SUV bitch" The dummy asked looking forward and not moving in any way.

"Doubt it; its Saturday the place looked quiet, wonder what bitch is doing there though?"

"Working out how to sell girls no doubt, remember when we followed her that time and she had the young girl in the car with her, wasn't the SUV but a smaller car. She went to that run down hotel out of town. When she came out she was alone, no girl. Obviously a drop off a trade or something" The dummy remembered telling Geoff who nodded yes.

"Well let's see what we can do" was all he said.

"You just keep in mind it quite easily could have been Cynthia, quite easily could of been her getting dropped off to a fucking psycho who bought her and used her and sells her to different men for pleasure you just remember that"

CHAPTER FIVE

Danny had taken the board out from under his bed and he and Geoff were sat on the floor in the early hours of the morning looking at it with a torch. Geoff was holding the torch in both hands and pointing it down towards the board, while Danny put the wooden pointer on its well worn surface. He put his fingers on the pointer and said in a low voice.

"I want to speak to you, are you there" Danny looked over at Geoff and smiled. Nothing happened so he repeated himself, but again nothing happened.

"What's wrong with it?" Geoff asked

"I am not sure, it normally talks to me" he frowned and tried again.

"Why are you not communicating, I want to talk to you are you there?"

"Maybe, it has gone out for a drink?" Geoff sniggered

"Shut up, you might be knocking it off, it is normally ok when you are not here" Danny looked at the board and tried again. But nothing was happening. He took his fingers off and sighed out in disappointment.

"Does it need batteries or something" Geoff mocked again.

But he stopped when he saw the wooden pointer suddenly move; he jumped back and looked at Danny who smiled at him with a grin of "I told you so" on his face.

The pointer moved to the letters W then H then O. Danny put his fingers back on the pointer.

"Who? Danny asked looking a little confused then said, oh he is my brother"

"Did you move that, you did it didn't you?" Geoff asked pointing the torch back down to the board once again.

"No I did not, the board does it and it talks to you, it gives you powers, you have seen what it has given me and there is much more I want and more it is going to give me it has said so"

"I don't like it, it is not natural Danny, let's stop, who are we talking too?"

"Shut up, you wimp, we are talking to the board, it is perfectly safe, I have been doing it for a while now and nothing bad has happened. It is a good board"

Geoff started to back off he was not sure and didn't like it, he didn't like to grip of fear in his body and the emptiness in his guts. And he didn't like the look of malevolence on his brother's face; he had not seen him look like this before, he had a wicked look about him.

"I don't know Danny it is not natural, is it evil?" Geoff asked his brother but not looking at him he had fixed his stare on the board in front of them on the floor.

"Shut up, come put your fingers on this pointer, put the torch in your mouth, that way you will shut up talking your shit, come on, do it" Danny snapped the command out at him.

Reluctantly Geoff did as he was told; he put the torch in his mouth and hesitantly put his fingers on the pointer. Danny then took over and stared back down at the board.

"Will you show us some of your power; show my brother what you can do"

The pointer moved and Geoff felt his heart miss a beat, he didn't know if Danny was moving it or what but he didn't like it. The pointer went to the word NO.

"Let's stop Danny, let's leave it now" Geoff said nervously taking the torch from his mouth.

"Oh you go to bed, it doesn't want to talk to you" Danny took the torch from him and pushed him away. He then turned his attention to the board and put the torch in his own mouth and put his fingers on the wooded pointer.

Geoff went off to bed and got snuggled under the covers; he laid on his side and watched Danny play with the board. The pointer seemed to be moving now and he was talking low and asking questions and the pointer was spelling out the answers.

He didn't know how long he was there because he fell asleep and when he awoke the next morning Danny was back in bed and the board hidden again.

"Danny, hey Danny" Geoff said but there was no answer. He got out of bed and opened the curtains to let the light of the morning fill the room. He then walked over to his brother and nudged him. But he didn't respond. He nudged him again and then pulled him over by his shoulder onto his back. He shook him and spoke his name again.

"Danny's eyes suddenly opened but they were white, solid white and his mouth dropped open as if he was going to speak but could not. Screaming Geoff backed off and fell over. He scrambled up and was going to dash out for door but stopped when Danny's voice said.

"Stop you idiot, what is wrong with you?" Geoff looked back and saw Danny sat on the edge of the bed looking normal but tired; he yawned and stretched his arms up then out.

"Are you ok, you were possessed or something" Geoff said shaking.

"Shut up, I am fine you are just an areshole"

"Is everything alright in there?" their mothers voice shouted out from the landing.

"Yes we are fine, Just Geoff having a bad dream" Danny shouted back.

"Well, keep the noise down" his mum said and then it was quiet.

"You are such a wimp Geoffrey, so weak and pathetic, you need to toughen up and become more of a man if you want to come with me, because I am going places" Danny stated and stood up and stretched out again yawning.

"I do not want to go anywhere, I think you need to get rid of that bloody board" Geoff told him while he stood by the door still holding the handle just in case.

"Then I will go myself, I offered you a chance, but you have decided not to take it, but let me tell you something Brother, if you tell anyone about this, and I mean anyone. The board will come for you. It told me last night. It doesn't like you and wants to hurt you, so there is only me stopping it, do you understand me?" his eyes were staring and his voice seemed very different, much more mature and definitely more menacing. He walked over to Geoff and came close to him and stared him in the eyes. He smiled a little then just pushed past him and walked out to the bathroom. Geoff didn't like it, he was shaking and didn't like that either. He looked down at the bed and knew the board was under it, the thought of destroying it crossed his mind but he didn't have the nerve. He just stood there and did nothing and when Danny came back he left the room and went to the bathroom.

They didn't talk much that day, and on their way home from school Danny walked a different way than Geoff did but they met up at the end of the street and walked into the house together so no one was any wise. The early evening went without incident but when they all settled down for the night Danny sat on the settee and just had a slight grin on his face. He kept making things move when no one was watching. They were all watching the TV and he turned the channel over, much to his Fathers annoyance who then started to bang the remote control in his hand and curse at it. Geoff noticed what he was doing and watched has he made an ornament move on the side board behind his mother. Turning to look at Geoff Danny smiled and his eyes widened and he opened his mouth flicking his tongue in and out.

Then the TV went bang and died, it made his mother jump and his father curse out loud. Geoff stared at Danny and shook his head, he could see what he was doing and didn't like it at all. Danny started to giggle.

"What the bloody hell are you laughing at lad" his father shouted at him annoyed.

"Nothing Father, nothing at all" Danny said standing up and headed off out of the room up to his room. Geoff followed him and left his parents shouting at each other and his mother blaming his Father of breaking the Television. Geoff could hear Danny laughing before he went into the room. He opened the door and gasped when he saw Danny hovering a few inches above the floor, and then spins in mid air and look at him. Geoff felt a force push him into the room and the door slammed behind him. He was petrified and didn't know what to do, he was shaking and tried to get out of the room but the door was closed solid and would not open. He pulled at the door handle but it was no good. He eventually turned to look at Danny who was still in mid air looking at him his head tilted to one said and wicked grin on his face, he was staring and made Geoff feel very uncomfortable.

"You do exactly what I say from now on, because I am no longer messing around, I am going to be getting the black magic power soon and nothing will ever stop me, nothing or no one"

"What do you mean, what is that?" Geoff said his voice quivering.

"Strong powerful magic" he smiled and took a deep breath. He came down and his feet were back on the floor, he walked up to Geoff and put his face next to his, Geoff could smell the horrid bad smell on his breath and it made him feel uncomfortable.

"You listen to me, from now on you do exactly what I say, I am selling my soul for the magic and when I get it I am unstoppable I will be able to do anything, to anyone" he sounded quite mad and not really in control.

"Danny, listen to me, it is not too late, we can get rid of the board and you will be back to normal we can go back to how we were" Geoff pleaded.

"What are you talking about, I do not want to go back to that shit, I am going into the realm of power and magic, that is what I want and that is what I am going to get. You had your chance and you were too weak and pathetic to take it" Danny was so different so angry and so evil Geoff could do nothing and he knew it.

"Ok, I will leave you alone, just don't hurt mum or dad" Geoff said backing off and holding back his fear and anxiety.

"Don't hurt mum or dad? Danny mocked in Geoff's voice, fucking pathetic, just get out of my way because if you don't you will be stamped into the ground" Danny pushed him out of the way and walked out of the room. He heard his parents arguing as he opened the door and he followed him out onto the landing and watched as he went down the stairs and out the front door. Running to the landing window he saw Danny heading off down the road and away from the house. Swallowing because his mouth was dry, Geoff was scared he didn't know what to do. He was shaking and sweating, he had never been so scared and he just didn't know what to do, he had taken Danny's threats seriously, he was seeing what Danny could do and he seemed to be getting stronger all the time. He could also see the entrapment he was going through the more he used the board the worse he was becoming. He walked back into the bedroom and looked down at Danny's bed; he knew the board was under there. He knew he had this one chance to destroy it. He closed the door and looked out of the window at where Danny had gone. He then knelt down and searched under the bed he looked under there but could not see it. He frantically searched and looked all round but could not find it. He looked round and went over to his bed the board was there under his own bed. He tried to pull the board but out suddenly it became heavy. He could not move it, it was like it was nailed to the floor, he tried and tried but it would not move. The wooden pointer was stuck on top of the board but he couldn't move this either. He sat down and kicked it with his foot but still the board would not budge.

He began to feel the tears dwell up inside, the frustration the fear it was all there and bubbling under the surface. He had no chance on moving the board, he lifted his bed up and stamped on it but it was unmovable and he just dropped the bed and burst into tears. He fell onto his own bed and sobbed. Cried into his pillow and just didn't know what to do.

He stayed there and was awake when Danny came home, he heard his Father shouting at him when he came back in. He waited for the bedroom door to open and he closed his eyes and pretended to be asleep. He heard Danny moving about and could sense he was on his knees reaching under his bed at one point. He dare not open his eyes. And he just kept them tight shut, and curled up under the covers. He was scared and he was worried, but he knew there was nothing he could do, no one to go too, he took everything Danny had said as the truth and he dare not risk what he would do if he did say something. So he was trapped, the board had taken control of his brother and there was nothing he could do about it.

****

The white SUV started up and the powerful engine purred with power and she pulled off and away out of the car park. The driver was a middle aged well dressed and well groomed woman. Her clothes were expensive and the jewellery she had on was even more so. She looked confident and professional. But if you looked closely at her eyes you would see there was false facade there. She had an evil and strong streak. If anyone crossed her they found that out. But you need to be strong and sometimes ruthless to be successful. She drove confident and fast and was good at it. She constantly was looking in her mirror and all round her, more than a normal person would, very cautious she was heading off to her large detached house. The house was expensive but it is paid for, she had a comfortable life and plenty of money. She enjoyed it and would let no one spoil that. There was no man in her life, not in a romantic way anyway. But there were women; she enjoyed women more than men.

She arrived home and entered the large electric gates that open automatically when she arrives; they close again behind her when she goes through. She looked round like a hawk as she drove up the drive. Stopping the car and turning the engine off, she stayed sat there for a moment. And scanned the whole surroundings before getting out of the SUV, then she got out and locked her vehicle. Went to her front door and opened the double locks on it. Went inside and closed and locked the door, with key and dead bolts on the inside of the door. She opened a small door on a cupboard at the side and keyed in her security number to turn off the alarm system. Throwing her small clutch bag on a small table she then sighed and felt safe. She took off her sling back shoes holding them in one hand and walked through into the large and clean and tidy living room. She dropped the shoes on the floor as she walked through into the open plan modern kitchen.

She was wearing an all in one dress and reached round to undo it behind her neck. Letting this hang down she opened the fridge and took out a bottle of water and went to sit on the large expensive leather couch. Lying across it she put her feet on one end and leaned her head on the arm rest of the other. She sipped her water and sighed out and started to close her eyes she was going to relax now and know she was safe. Her house is secure she is locked in and is safe; it always makes her feel good. Closing her eyes fully she took some deep breaths and then sipped her water. She was tired and she needed a long hot bath and then some wine and a good night's sleep. She had been on edge since the Agent was found hung; she knew it was not suicide. Everyone who knew him thought the same; she was playing it low at the moment. Better to be safe than sorry she thought. She put the bottle of water down and relaxed back she was not sleeping to good at nights. And now she felt tired and like she often did she drifted off to sleep the couch. The house was secure and it was the only place she felt safe at the moment. The only place she could relax and be secure, it had been a crazy time and a worrying time she was trying to relax and she hoped she soon would be calm again.

She was awoke suddenly by hearing her phone ringing in her bag by the door, she got up and walked casually to go get it, there was no rush in her movement at all. She opened her bag and pulled the phone out. She looked at the number before answering.

"Yes what is it?" she said in a very eloquent voice, which oozed intelligence and breeding.

"I have what you wanted me to get for you" the woman's voice on the other end said

"Well aren't we a clever girl, there is hope for you yet, right you keep it safe I will be in touch when I want you to bring it to me do you understand?" she asked in a very condescending manner and tone.

"Yes miss I do, I will not let you down" the voice chirped back.

"Well if you ever do it would be the last thing you ever did" her voice was cold and merciless and heartless. She had no expression on her face as she was talking.

"I appreciate all you have done for me I will not let you down"

"Yes, you have already said that, let us see how well you handle this and see how much you really want to please me shall we?" he voice changed to a lower tone in mid sentence.

"Anything, I will do anything you want" the voice said willingly.

"What a wonderful logic you have. Anything I want? Well I will hold you to that"

"Anything, I want to please you and do well"

"Right, stop sounding pathetic and we shall see what happens, just let me warn you this once, if you ever cross me if anything ever goes wrong, you will disappear and end up where the rest of them do , is that understood?

"Yes, yes I understand" she said nervously

"Good now go away and leave me alone" she pressed the off button and walked back into her front room. She went back and lay back down on the settee. Holding her phone up, she pressed through and found a number. She rang it and waited, and waited then it was answered by a man's voice.

"Is it all good?" is all he said.

"Seems so, I have a shipment for you soon, as we agreed and what you are looking for"

"Excellent, I am pleased and so will my colleagues I am sure"

"We have a new deliver person too, so all clean and all good for us" she said

"That is good to hear, and have you heard anything about our other departed partner?"

"No, nothing, case closed, but we still have to be very careful with shipments"

"Agreed, better safe than sorry can't have anything going astray, I am pleased thank you it is a pleasure doing business"

"I will be in touch when we are ready to deliver" she hung up the phone and a smile came across her face. She stretched out and slipped out of her dress. She let it fall on the floor and walked off up stairs undressing as she did. She went to the bathroom and turned on the gold taps in to a large porcelain bath tub. Reaching over she took a bottle of expensive bath salts from the side and dropped a few into the hot water that was rushing from the tap and crashing into the bath tub. She then took the rest of her clothes off and stood looking at her naked self in the full length mirror on the tiled wall. Turning around she looked at her body. Inspecting herself and smiling she liked her fit and healthy body. It was perfect in her eyes and she is so proud it is all real, nothing fake about any of it, she was firm and fit. When the bath tub filled she eased herself into the hot water and gasped for a moment then settled down, relaxing.

"So when are we going to grab her?" The dummy insisted to Geoff they were both sat on the settee and facing each other.

"We have to be careful and play this very safe, I can't just keep turning up in my car every day waiting for her, there are cameras and I will be noticed straight away"

"Details, bloody details, we did before we use to follow that fat Bastard do you remember, we even followed her in the SUV a for a bit" the dummy insisted

"Yes I know but they were unaware then, they will all be on edge now, more vigilant and this girl will probably be scared out of her wits"

"Poor cow I must say" the dummy mocked unfeelingly.

"Stop rushing that is how mistakes are made I am not doing this until I know we can get away with it, so stop trying to rush it along" Geoff insisted.

"It is alright for you, this is all I have all I have to keep me going" the dummy said turning its head and lifting its eye brows over and over.

"So what the hell you going to do when all this is over, because I am telling you this is it, no more after this, no matter what you say"

"Well then we need to go into show business, we would make a great double act" the dummy said in a jokingly fashion.

"I am serious, this is the end, finished no more after this" Geoff insisted

The dummy went still and its head jolted to the side and looked at Geoff straight away, it said nothing for a while then the jaw dropped open and back again.

"But what if I like it, what if you like it?" The dummy said quietly

"I do not like it and won't ever like it, this is the last time" Geoff insisted.

"We shall see, we shall see" the dummy said in a matter of fact tone

"No, we shall not see, I am telling you once and for all this is the last time" Geoff shouted.

"Ah I saw your lips move" the dummy rolled back and chuckled and its mouth opened and closed a few times. But Geoff was not impressed. He shook his head and stood up he left the room going out to the toilet. When he returned the dummy was sat in the chair its arms resting on chairs armrests and its legs crossed. It followed Geoff round the room with a stare as he went to the kitchen area. It was looking at him all the while and eventually Geoff came in and stood in front of it saying in a raised voice.

"You can do the silent stare all you want, this is the last one the end, so just live with it. No more after this" Geoff pointed his finger at the dummy as he spoke. The dummy said nothing and just looked at him, and carried on doing so when he went back into the kitchen. Geoff made himself a drink and brought it back out. The dummy was gone and Geoff didn't care where. He sat down and turned the TV on and started to flick through the channels when suddenly the TV turned off by its self. He sighed out and shook his head.

"Dummy, stop being a wanker and stop messing about with the TV" as soon a she said it the TV came back on by its self.

"You can sulk all you want, you have to come to terms with it, we did alright before and will again, so stop being a wooden head or I will come in there and give you wood worm" Geoff shouted out knowing it was probably in the bed room.

"That would not be very nice" the dummy shouted from the other room.

"I am sure you would live with it" Geoff shouted back

"You have a nasty streak in you sometimes Geoffrey and I like that version of you better then the wimp you are now"

"Whatever, it doesn't change a thing" Geoff said as he still flicked through the channels on the TV but not finding anything he wanted to watch.

"Well it should change everything"

"And why is that?" Geoff closed his eyes in a moment of temper and sighed out loud as the TV turned off by its self again. He threw the remote on the settee next to him.

"Because you have a short memory, you tend to forget things, I on the other hand forget nothing, and you would be wise to remember that oh Great one" the voice was mocking but very serious and Geoff didn't like it.

"So you keep saying, but to be honest I don't want to remember everything and you can bring the past up as much as you like it is not going to change a thing"

"You have to go to sleep" was the chilling reply.

Geoff said nothing and could not help but face the memory that had bolted its self from his subconscious into his conscious brain. He sighed and leaned back on the settee. He didn't answer he didn't need too.

***

Danny had become very distant and even more so today, it was the weekend and they would normally out playing and exploring and doing their magic tricks. But today Danny was sat in his room; he didn't want any contact with anyone. His mother had been up to talk to him but got nowhere, Geoff didn't want to go talk to him but told his mother he had done and that he was just not feeling well. His dad left him alone and told everyone else to do the same.

The day was quiet; Danny didn't eat anything and didn't talk to anyone. Geoff went out for a long walk he didn't feel happy in the house any more. Not knowing what he knew and he feared for his parents. He just didn't know what to do. He walked through the woods and into the small town he spent most of the afternoon there. On his way home he had a slight panic attack and had to sit down. He just did not want to spend another night sleeping in the same room as his brother or that board. The more he thought about it the more anxious he became. He had not been sleeping well at all and he was tired all the time. The fear inside him was eating him away and wearing him down. He didn't want to become ill but he could see it going that way. He got up from the little wall he was sat on and headed back home. He arrived late afternoon and walked in. The house seemed hollow somehow it always felt like home and warm and safe to him. But today it felt empty of life almost. His mother was making some food in the Kitchen and his Dad was in the garden shed. He went down and sat in the living room on the settee. He looked at the big new Television they had bought but was not interested in watching it somehow. He had lost interest in everything. And could feel depression in his mind, he just didn't know what to do and was scared to do anything.

He stayed there until the food was ready, Danny was asked to come down but he refused and stayed in his room. The meal went silently and Geoff helped his mother to wash the dishes after, while Dad watched the new TV.

When it got late, and Geoff knew he had to go to bed soon. He began to feel the palms of his hands sweat. He started to breath heavier and felt a panic coming over him.

"Ok, lad its time you were in bed" His dad said not taking his eyes from the TV screen.

Geoff stood up and wished them both good night; he stayed brave and left the room. He stood at the bottom of the stairs and looked up. He swallowed and took a deep breath. Slowly he walked up the stairs and went into the bathroom and brushed his teeth.

He walked to the bedroom door and froze; he was scared to go in. But eventually he slowly turned the handle and opened the door. The room was dark except for a side light next to his own bed; Danny was in bed and looked sound asleep. He looked round the room and nothing looked out of place. It was a bit of a relief to him and he breathed out. He slowly went in and closed the door he was staying very quiet and sneaked about getting undressed. He slipped into bed and pulled the covers up over him. He decided to leave the side light on, it made him feel much safer not being in total darkness. It was silent and he looked round the room. It was his room, the same room he had plenty of happy times. He and Danny had made it their magic kingdom at one time. But lately it was more of a tormented darkness. He closed his eyes and tried to sleep. His body wanted it but his mind would not allow it. It was a constant battle between mind and body. Eventually his body won and he drifted off and fell into an uneasy sleep. He had no idea how long he had been asleep but when he opened his eyes he was shocked into fear. Leaning over him was Danny. Staring with white eyes, right at him, a demented looking smile on his face and he was only about a foot away from his face just staring and not moving. Geoff shook with fear and didn't know what to do, he just shook uncontrollably. Then without a word being said Danny backed off and got back into bed.

Geoff looked over and saw his brother asleep as if nothing had happened. He shook his head and thought for a moment he had been dreaming, but no, it was real he was stood there and his eyes were total white like there was no eye ball in them. The room seemed heavy and stifling he found it harder to breath. He was gasping for air at one point but dare not move out of his bed; he kept looking over at his brother. Then it was gone, it was like everything that was wrong was gone. The air was light again the atmosphere was easy the light shone by his bed side all was quiet. He took deep breaths and looked round the room, all seemed normal all seemed safe just like it use too. He looked over to his brother who seemed to be sleeping peacefully.

He was confused and didn't know what to do, eventually he plucked up the courage to get out of bed, he looked under it first then over again to his brother. He slowly and quietly put his feet on the floor and stood up. Looking round the room he took a deep breath and walked the short distance to his brother's bed. He swallowed and gathered all his courage. He put his hand on his brother's shoulder and then jumped back with a start as Danny turned and looked at him saying in his normal can regular voice.

"What is it, what is wrong?" He turned around and sat up.

"You ok, you feeling alright?" Geoff said a little confused but very much relived.

"Yes I am fine, why what is it?" Danny looked confused and frowned at his brother.

"Nothing I just thought you were, err, you know, well its fine good" he said and didn't make sense but was lost for words anyway.

"Shut up you Looney and go to sleep" Danny turned back around pulling the covers over himself then and was quiet and still.

Geoff went back to bed and did the same, he wondered if it was a bad dream after all, he convinced himself it was, this made him feel better so he was going to stick with that explanation. He didn't get any more sleep that night but at least nothing else happened.

Danny seemed much better the next day, much more responsive to his family and more like his old self. His mum was pleased about it and his dad grunted his approval. They put it down to him just having an off day, not feeling too well. But Geoff still knew something was not right. He knew his brother better than anyone and he knew Danny was not he old Danny of before. No matter how much he seemed to be like it there was still something wrong. But for now it was better to have him like this so he went along with it. Sunday was always a slow and easy day and the rain was coming down outside so it was a day in for them all.

Even though all seemed safe, Geoff was still reluctant to be alone with his brother. Danny was in high spirits and seemed happy. But Geoff was not going to fall into any trap of false sense of security. He played alone in front of his parents and all seemed well. They spent the day watching TV or reading Geoff helped his mum prepare dinner and Danny went to the shed with his dad. Which in its self was a rare thing, not only because of Danny taking the time to do so, but for their dad to allow anyone into the shed anyway, it was his little man cave and his domain. You needed permission to enter and had to touch nothing while you were in there. After dinner dad fell asleep in his chair and snored. Danny went up to his room and Geoff helped his mother to wash up and put away.

"You and Danny alright love?" his mother asked him while they were drying the pots

"Yeah, fine why?" Geoff asked

"You both seem a little distant from each other, have you had a fall out?"

"No, we are fine, just doing our own thing, all is good mum" Geoff smiled and took a plate from her she had just washed and dried it with his tea towel.

"Mum do you know what the most common owl is in England?" Geoff asked.

"Oh I don't know the barn owl?" his mum suggested

"Nope, try again"

"The tawny owl that is a very popular" his mum said expectantly.

"Nope, it is the teat" Geoff said.

"Teat? Teat owl"

Geoff looked at her and waited for the penny to drop, but it was a long time coming, she shook her head and didn't get it.

"Teat owl, tea towel mum" Geoff explained.

She finally got the joke and giggled. They finished up and came back into the main room. Dad was snoring away in the chair and all seemed like a normal lazy Sunday. Geoff sat on the settee for a short while then plucked up the courage to go up to his room and see Danny.

He walked slowly up the stairs and hesitated by the door. He listened and could hear nothing so slowly he opened the door and went in. Danny was sat on his bed with a deck of cards in his hand. He looked up and smiled at Geoff as he came in.

"Have you done the dishes like a good little boy" he said jokingly

"It's your turn next time" Geoff said sitting on his own bed.

"It is a woman's job, so you are better suited" Danny said laughing

"Shut up, you dummy" Geoff said feeling a bit more comfortable in the fact that his brother was more like normal.

"I have been thinking I am not going to use the board any more" Danny said looking down at the cards in his hands.

"I am glad about that, it is too dangerous Danny" Geoff suddenly felt a great weight lift from his shoulders and a relief in his whole body.

"I know, it was very easy and friendly at first, but it is getting nasty now and demanding" he said putting the cards down and interlocking his fingers. He was looking down at his hands and Geoff could see he was scared and nervous about something.

"Well, let's get rid of it, we could go and do it now, the rain has stopped" Geoff suggested.

"It won't let us, it is not going to let me go" Danny said looking down at his hands and started to fidget his fingers. Geoff could see he was worried and came over to sit next to him on the bed. Danny looked up at him and Geoff looked back telling him as he did.

"Look you dummy, we will go and destroy the damn thing, and we could take it into Dad's shed cut into a thousand pieces. Bur it, do anything but we have to do it"

"You can try, but I do not want to use it anymore Geoff, it is bad and it is scaring me" Danny was genuinely scared and Geoff had never seen him like this before.

"Let's go throw it in the river, we can take it now and throw it far out into the water and never see it again" Geoff put his arm round his brother and tried to sound confident, but he was still worried and knew something had to be done soon.

"It won't let us, it has given me powers, and now wants something in return, I can't just throw it away it will come back and find me, it has said so"

"What the board speaks to you?" Geoff was getting confused.

"It has a spirit attached to it, I have to let that spirit go or it will kill me" Danny took a deep breath and his breathing became irregular.

"Let it go, what do you mean, let it go?"

"I have to die so it can live" Danny shook his head and started to get upset.

"Listen, you can't believe what it tells you, it might just be lying to get what it wants, so let's at least try and get rid of it" Geoff didn't know how much of this was what he has been told, or what Danny was assuming but he did know this was his chance to get his brother back. He was going to do whatever he could to help him and sort this out.

"What are we going to do?" Danny said looking up at his Brother with regret and fear in his eyes. He was not having fun anymore and was frightened and confused.

"Right, where is it, let's get it and see if we can smash it" Geoff said looking round.

Danny got off the bed and reached under it, he pulled the board out and put it on his bed. Geoff looked at it and watched as Danny backed away from it looking down at it with dread in his eyes. Looking round the room Geoff found an old school bag he didn't use anymore. He opened it and Danny put the board and wooden pointer in the bag. They both put a jacket on and headed off out to the river. They left the house and when they go to the road they started to run, Geoff carrying the bag and Danny running behind as they raced away. They both felt good and started to laugh; finally they had got the board out of the house and now were going to get rid of it. They both dashed across the road and down the dirt track over the small fence and across the field. It was just like the old times both Brothers running and out on an Adventure they both felt good and it was great Geoff thought. They finally came to the river that ran through the town. They knew where to go as they have played there many times. It was a pretty place and picturesque the river ran through the town and away joining a larger one a few miles away. They came to the river bank and stopped. Both out of breath Geoff threw the bag on the ground and stamped on it. Danny did the same thing they both laughed and jumped up and down on the bag with the board inside. Looking round Geoff grabbed a rock. He was going to open the bag but Danny stopped him. He didn't want to see the board again. So Geoff just pounded the rock into the bag and hoped he smashed the board as he did so. Then picking it up, he looked round. Danny looked around again and nodded. He picked his spot right in the centre. He pulled his arm back and threw the bag hard and high it flew through the air and landed with a slash into the centre of the river. It floated for a few moments then the current took it a little way and it sank.

Both boys put their hand up in the air and cheered, screaming out with joy and happiness they hugged and danced round. It was gone finally it was gone and they could get back to normal again. Geoff was so happy and Danny was so relived. They ran from the place and headed off back home. They walked quickly and were cheerful about what they had done. It seemed to of lifted their spirits and both boys were chatting happily when they got back in. They took their shoes off and went up stairs to their room. Both boys froze for a moment and were thinking the same thing.

"What, if." Geoff said looking at Danny with a sudden worried face

"I know, what will we do" Danny said holding the door handle and they both dare not move for a moment. Then slowly he went in follow by Geoff the room was just as they left it. They both let out a sigh of relief but still searched the room anyway, under the beds and in the draws and cupboard, everywhere. The board was gone nowhere to be seen. They then both lay on their beds and just started to laugh with relief and a calmness of solace came over them. Breathing out Danny rubbed his face he was so happy to be rid of the board.

"We did it, we bloody did it" Geoff said triumphantly

"Yes we did, thank you Geoff" Danny said smiling.

"It's ok you dummy just don't do anything like that again" Geoff stated and shook his head and started to laugh once again it was a great release for them both.

"I know, I am sorry brother I won't" Danny told him

"And don't make your eyes go white like that again it scared the shit out of me" Geoff said

"What do you mean I didn't?" Danny said confused with no memory of anything of the kind.

"Yeah, yeah just don't do it again it is not right and too bloody scary"

Both boys were tired and had an early night they both fell asleep pretty quickly and all was quiet and easy in the room again. Mother and Father were down stairs watching their new Television and all seemed normal for several hours. But unbeknown to them there was something not right at all. Something very wrong, the room had become heavy and the air thicker it seemed. It was sending them both to sleep quickly and neither of them noticed. It didn't take long before they were both fast asleep. Dad in his chair and mum on the settee leaned back. It was getting late and it was dark and quiet outside. The house was locked up and secure. Both boys were fast asleep and their room was lit by a small table lamp on Geoff's side. This flickered and went out, but they didn't notice. The room's atmosphere became heavy like before the air got thinner and Danny wok up with a shock, like a shot of electricity had just shocked through his body. He was still asleep but he was sat up. His eyes opened and they were white. He stood up and walked over to his brother and stared down at him for a few moments. Then he walked to the window and opened it. He looked out and then down at the drop to the concrete below. He didn't hesitate and climbed up onto the window sill. He looked down and then diver head first straight into the concrete below. Smashing his skull and breaking the neck, he was bleeding badly and no one knew, no one saw what happened and no one heard anything. He was found by his dad the next day, lying where he fell in a large pool of blood he was dead, his body already cold.

CHAPTER SIX

She was scared and she knew a lot, too much for her own good and she was very aware of this fact. When she work for the Agent as he secretary she knew he had some bad goings on she knew he was a dirty Bastard but the job was easy and good money. She didn't enjoy fucking him or giving him sexual favours but it was all part of the job she thought and when a deal went down, she was rewarded pretty well for part and her silence afterwards. But her new boss was not as easy to please; she was known to be horrid and vicious and callous.

She didn't have a choice, she had to go work for her she was ordered too and dare not resist. She knew that she knew too much, and she also knew that she was in danger if she ever gave them any kind of hint she was going run or talk to anyone. She was stuck and there was nothing she could or dare do about it. She had got what the Boss had wanted and she had secured delivery, it was all done in secret but in plain sight disguised as something else. She had dealt with a third party who instructed her and she did what she was told. Now She had been given furthur instructions to drive a car and leave it somewhere. Under no circumstances was she to look in the boot, even if she heard noises. She was to drive it to a specific place and leave it and walk away. If she got pulled over by the police she was instructed what to say and if they searched the car she was told to get away anyway she could. But if she ever told on them she would be dead, and no where would be safe for her. No matter what the police offered or told her. She knew all this was not false threats she knew they were powerful and could and did make people disappear.

Waiting for her phone to ring several days later she was anxious and also scared. This was her first solo job and she had to get it right. She put out of her mind what she was doing and what she was carrying. She just wanted to make sure she does the job right. This was where she was going to make her real money the secretary front in the offices was nothing more than that. She sat there and looked the part. It was a way to keep a leach on her and under control. Her new boss sacred her, she scared everyone and the horrible stories they she had heard, mostly from her old Agent boss, she knew to be true. The woman was cruel and didn't care about anyone but herself. She had been dealing in human traffic for years and made lots of money out of it. She got girls and boys and sold them for hard cash, she was good at it, she had a network of individuals who groomed and got her victims. Just like the agent did, she had very powerful friends and knew some very nasty people, she was definitely someone you didn't or dare not double cross. Coming to terms with all this and seeing that as the bad side of this situation she knew she was in, she knew she would be paid pretty well for her part. Why should be bothered, she didn't know any of these girls, it was nothing to her. It was a way to make money and stay alive. Self preservation in this line of work was paramount.

She jumped and her phone jumped out of her hand as she was startled, she was sat on her little bed in her little apartment, she picked up the phone and said

"Hello" she already knew who it was.

"It is set and you are doing it, do exactly what we discussed and do it to the letter is that understood. Keep to the time table. I will ring you and if you have not delivered or you do not answer or anything goes wrong, then your employment will be terminated do I make myself clear?" her voice was callous and cold, direct and menacing.

"Yes I understand, I will not let you down"

The phone went dead and she knew this was it, that night she had to go get a car that was parked up in a warehouse, she had to drive it somewhere leave it and walk away that simple. That is what she focused on, she put out of her mind what might be in the boot she was not bothered all she was doing was driving a car somewhere and then walking away. The car had been driven here by some just like her and now she had to drive it someone else. She stood up and looked at the small clock on the bed side cabinet. She had four hours to kill before she had to go out and do this. Just four hours before she had to prove herself, four hours before she had to make the delivery and then she was hooked in and could never leave, she would always be an accessory. This is how they got you how they controlled you. She paced up and down looking at the clock again; she was becoming agitated and rubbed her hands together. Four hours and she could get going; she took deep breaths and sat back sown then laid flat on the bed looking up. She sighed out loud and closed her eyes. But her mind was never going to let her rest or sleep. She looked over at the clock again and took a deep breath pushing the air out of her mouth making her cheeks come out as she did. Just four hours, that is all she had she sat back up and glanced at the clock again.

Geoff had got lucky the day before, very lucky indeed, he was parked on the road but out of sight by the office block and he saw the secretary leaving in her car. It was a stroke of luck and that is all it was. He was losing faith in his ability to find the woman but here she was driving past him at this moment. He followed at a discreet distance and found out where she lived. It was one step closer to getting to who they really wanted. He noted the address and could see it was a rundown apartment block building and pretty easy to just walk in and not be noticed if you were careful. Everyone minded their own business and pretty much it was a quiet place and no one was bothered about anyone else who lived there, they just kept themselves to themselves and this suited Geoff right down to the ground. He didn't really have a plan, his mind changed day by day about the whole thing. Someday she wanted to just move on and forget it other days he was all for it and wanted to make them suffer. But at least now they had a starting place to work something out. Geoff was getting frustrated with the Dummy's insistence of going in there all guns blazing and making them suffer. He was trying very hard to sort out a plan that was safe and secure. He was no expert at this but was trying the best he could. He did think the best way to the SUV bitch was through this secretary and that was the way they were going to go. She had been easy last time to hypnotise and control he just hoped she would be again.

"I do not know if I can make her actually go do something without me being there to control her line of thought" Geoff tried to explain to the Dummy.

"You are making excuses, you can do it, I have seen you do it before"

"No you have not, there is a difference in mind control and hypnosis, and they are different things completely" Geoff explained

"You hypnotise her and she will do what you ask her?" the Dummy stated strongly

"Wrong, Mind control is gradual, you have to work with and break down the person you are trying to take over and brainwash, and it is mind control when you are controlled by someone or something like a trigger, music, or colour, but it all takes time to do it, it doesn't just happen. I can't go there and hypnotise her and made her do what I want when I want"

"You made her before, you made her forget" The dummy was getting agitated and shaking in the chair as it was talking to Geoff who was sat on the settee turned to face it.

"That is more power of suggestion; I can hypnotise up to an extent but not mind control"

"This is bollocks; you are just shying away again, trying to get out of it"

"No, I am not, the best we can hope for is to get information out of her, she will not just be able to take us to, or do anything to the bitch we really want, she will just have to be a means to an end and that is all we can hope for" Geoff turned and sat straight on the settee taking his gaze off the dummy who was now moving erratically over and over.

"Let me confront her I will get the information and I will make her do what we want and need I am not afraid like you" The dummy spouted out quickly with annoyance.

"We will work out a plan and we will pay her a visit and try and get all the information we can out of her, I will put her under and we will see what we get" Geoff stated and was not going to be moved on the decision.

"I will go with you and we will work on her together, she knows and she is involved so she should be made to pay" The dummy had settled and was not as agitated.

"We will pay her a visit and see what she has to say, but I can only do so much so do not expect miracles. We will just have to see what happens, because we know nothing about what the set up is with them two yet"

"Yes we do, she worked for fat Agent fucker, now she works for SUV bitch, what else do you need to make the connection?" The dummy shook its head and the jaw dropped open closing with a snap again a little time after. They continued to argue and discus the situation into the night. Both having their opinion and both having the anger dwell up about the other.

While all this was going on the Secretary was walking along the road by the back of her apartment she was on her way. Dressed in jeans and a woolly top and had a light jacket on. She headed to the warehouse she had been instructed to pick the car up from. She still had half an hour to go but it was a twenty minute walk at least. She was breathy heavy and nervous, she hoped she would not chicken out, she knew she could not afford to if she wanted to live. It was only a car, and a drive that is what she kept saying to herself, it was only a job and it was going to be over soon, just drive the car leave it and get back home. Simple and easy, that is what she was concentrating on right now. She double checked she had some money in her jacket pocket; she needed it to get back home and planned on taking a bus.

Walking steady and took deep breaths and kept the negative thoughts out of her head, all the "what ifs" and what could go wrong, what if the car was not there, or anything went wrong. She had fought with these thoughts for the past four hours or so, but now she was getting focused and going to just drive this car leave it and come home, that simple. Heading out to the trading estate and could see the warehouses were she was going too, she checked her little cheap watch she had on her wrist, still ten minutes to pick up. She slowed down and wanted to arrive right on time. Didn't want to see anyone drop off or didn't want anyone to see her pick up. She swallowed and sighed out nervously. Heading towards the warehouse she checked her watch again. It was almost time for her pickup she looked round and could see everywhere was deserted.

No one around, or no cameras it seemed. This probably was why they used this place, quiet and deserted at night time.

She double checked the time and this was it, she repeated to herself the instructions, large warehouse at the end, number four, big large on the side, she saw this and headed towards it, so far so good she thought. Searching round all the time as she walked and go to the warehouse she sighed out. There was to be a small door at the right hand side of the two large doors on the front, she came round and saw it. She went to this and opened it slipping inside as she did. The warehouse was cold and large and not lit at all. She took a little torch out of her side jacket pocket, she had been told to bring one. Shining it into the darkness she suddenly got scared the size of the place frightened her. It was a big wide open space and she felt like she was the only person alive on earth at that time. She shivered and looked round for the car. It was parked towards the back and by a roller door back entrance. She walked through the warehouse and was fighting a panic attack as she did. She didn't like it she felt vulnerable and nervous. The place was huge and had some sort of storage all the way to the back but she couldn't tell what it was. It was palliated up and stacked on racks. Her shoes made a loud noise on the concrete flooring has she made her away across the place and she started to tip toe and increase her speed. She finally reached the car. It was an old but large Ford. She looked inside it was empty and she could see the keys in the ignition. Looking up she went to the door and pulled a loop chain on the side the roller door started to lift up as she did. It made a very loud noise and she stopped for moment shaking. Looking round thinking someone would come to investigate the noise. She breathed heavy then carried on she only took the door high enough to get the car out. Then dashing quickly into it she started the vehicle up, it kicked into life straight away and she slowly drove it out into the yard area. Going back into the warehouse she closed the steel roller doors by pulling the loop chain the opposite way they came down and sat snugly on the ground. She then searched round for the exit door to the side. Going through this she ran to the car and quickly drove away putting her light on. She sighed out with relief and was on her way.

She settled into the old worn seat and pulled the seat belt round clicking it into place, reaching under the seat she searched for and found the bar to pull to move the seat forward. Then she was happy and set she drove carefully and headed off to where she had to leave the car for the next pick up. She could hear nothing from the back and was glad about it. She put it all from her mind and just concentrated on driving to the stone bridge which was a half hour drive away at least. Breathing out through her mouth she sighed and did a slight nervous giggle of relief. Easy she thought, no problem, she drove and settled back getting use to the large size and power of this car, much bigger and older and noisier then her little one. But she soon got the hang of it and headed away happier now it was almost done. She kept trying to listen for a sound from the back but she didn't want to hear one. Somehow she could not stop herself from trying to hear one though. Soon she was approaching the bridge, it was a dirt road and she struggled to drive down it. She put her full beam on and slowed down being careful as she manoeuvred through the pot holes and uneven ground. She could see the old stone bridge in the distance. Pulling up to it she slowed and then came to a stop on the bridge its self. This road and bridge was pretty deserted and obviously not used much. She stopped on the bridge and turned off the engine. She left the car and walked away back where she had come. Using her little torch as light until she got out onto the main road again where there were street lights, she didn't look back and did everything exactly as she had been instructed. She knew she was probably being watched but was not bothered the car would be gone soon and the merchandise in the back sold and or delivered. She didn't care she had done her bit and now was on her way home. Walking steady she finally got back onto the main road and headed for the bus stop she had passed, she was looking out for them all the time she had been driving along. She just had to figure out which bus to catch now to get back home. This was her first run so they probably would arrange transport for future drop offs she thought to herself, it was not too bad and she had done it, she smiled and was pleased with herself.

It was late when she got in and she was late getting up the next morning, she rushed into work and settled down into her chair by her unimpressive and small desk. No sooner had she done this then her phone rang and she was summoned instantly to her new Bosses office. A sense of fear struck her core, she shivered and became nervous. What if something had gone wrong, what if she was now to be asked some questions she could not answer. He did everything to the letter she got the car and delivered it. She nervously got up and walked to the lift; she got in and pressed the top floor button. It didn't take long and she walked down the lush carpeted floor to the end and largest office on the floor. She swallowed took a deep breath and composed herself. Then knocked twice and waited.

"Enter" was the command from inside.

She opened the door and walked into the large and well kept office, the desk was very large and kept immaculately tidy and clean. Just like the rest of the office. There were framed certificates on the walls and the carpet was so thick and expensive you almost sank into it as you walked along. She walked up to the desk and with a very worried look on her face stood there, her shoulders hunched slightly and her eyes tearing up, she was shaking uncontrollably and waited for whatever was going to come at her.

"You delivered last night as we said, was there any problems did anyone see you?" Her new boss said looking her straight in the eye and knowingly making her nervous.

"No, all went well no one followed and I didn't see anyone at all" she said with a quiver in her voice and she nodded with a weak smile.

"Stop being pathetic girl, I am simply asking you some questions about the delivery"

"Yes, I am sorry, all went well it was all good" she looked at the expensive top and short skirt her boss was wearing. She was made up perfectly and looked a million dollars as they say.

"Good, you did alright I suppose for your first time, so you say you saw no one, nothing strange or out of the ordinary?" she said shifting in her chair and leaning forward to expose her cleavage but kept her gaze towards her eyes.

"I saw no one, I just did what i was told it all went well with no problems, I just want to please you and will do everything right" she said calming herself a little.

Mmmm, will you now, well I will put that to the test then shall I?" she leaned back and clasped her hands behind her head pushing her chest out and keeping eye contact all the time she did it, then came back down and resumed her cleavage showing position.

"Yes I am a good worker and will do anything"

"You keep looking at my tits don't you?" she said calmly

"No, no sorry, I..." she looked away and was embarrassed.

"It is alright you can look at them, do you like them" she said forcing her to look back with a stare and the tone of her voice.

"You are a very beautiful woman miss" she said with an edgy smile.

"I am all real too, nothing fake about me" she said proudly

"No, I can see that Miss" she agreed nervously

"And you want to please me and do anything, you said?"

"Yes, I will always do my best"

"Come on then show me" She pushed back on her chair and opened her legs, she lifted her short skirt up exposing herself, she was not wearing any underwear.

"I, I don't understand?" She said confused and worried.

"Come and fucking pleasure me now you little bitch, on your knees and crawl here and eat me, you are mine now and you better get use to the fact, and you better be good"

Shaking she looked round then took a deep breath; she walked around to the side of the desk and knelt down. She looked up at the Boss who was looking down at her with her legs wide open and a glint of wickedness in her eye. She slowly moved towards her and looked up as she got close. The Boss looked down and nodded eagerly for her to do it. Her head went between the legs and she pleasured her, she did it well and the Boss grabbed the back of her head pulling her into herself and twisted her fist in her hair pulling her deep in and not letting her go until she was finished and satisfied. Then she lifted her head up and slapped her hard around the face before throwing her off and onto the floor, standing up she pulled her skirt down and straighten herself up, then sitting back down and didn't even look at the secretary again but told her with a nasty voice.

"Right get out and go do some work, I will call if I want that again, just remember who you work for and who fucking owns your pathetic little life now"

She shakily stood up off the floor and left the office; she wiped her mouth and headed for the ladies toilets, and cleaned herself up. She washed her face and rinsed her mouth out then looked at herself in the mirror and started to cry uncontrollably. She sobbed and put her head in her hands and didn't know how to stop herself from shaking. She felt used and frightened and knew she was now trapped for good, she had just been shown the fact and taught that lesson for sure, she would be used as and when wanted, she also knew she had to please the Boss good, because if not there would be the real risk of her being passed on to others who would use and abuse her at will. The thought made her cry more and she tried to compose herself. She was tired and felt sick but knew she would have to get back to the desk. She shook her head and took deep breaths to calm herself and then set about making herself look presentable and hide the fact she had been crying and upset. She did the best she could and bravely walked back to her desk and her mediocre job that had been invented for her to keep her close, and she now knew used and abused too. The rest of the day went slowly, she was always in fear of a phone call for her to go back up to the boss's office but it never came. She was so very tired and by the afternoon was struggling to keep her eyes open. The night had been so long and it was such a long and tiring journey back by bus, then she couldn't sleep and when she got up she was rushed and tired and running late. It had all taken its toll on her well being and her nerves. She had been worrying all day and now was exhausted. So looked like what she was, very tired and run down. She finally signed off shut down her computer and headed out and towards home. She got into her little car and drove off trying to keep her eyes open as she did. A sudden tiredness had come over her and her body and mind needed rest, driving she just had tunnel vision and wanted her bed. She wasn't even going to eat she was so tired and exhausted.

"I am wearing a mask this time" Geoff said while he sat in the car just outside the apartment block waiting for the secretary to return.

"What the hell for?" the dummy asked laid flat in its box on the back seat.

"I just am, just in case I am noticed. Geoff said not looking back but still out of the front windscreen and waiting.

"Stupid, you are going to erase her mind you daft idiot she won't remember a thing"

"Well maybe not but I am wearing one" Geoff insisted.

"Stupid" was all, the dummy said.

"Precaution that is what it is" Geoff defended

"Stupid, we are supposed to be blindfolding her, remember, and then you do your hypnosis bit before we leave anyway" The dummy shook its head, dropping its jaw open.

"We should be in there by now, come on she will be home soon" Geoff got out of the car and took the suitcase with dummy in out from the back. He locked his car and walked the short distance towards the apartments. They were dirty and people were not proud to live here. New faces come and went so they were paid no attention, it is always best to mind your own business in this type of neighbourhood anyway. Geoff got to the door and easily manipulated the latch lock with a strong piece of plastic pushed into the crack of the door and releasing the lock, the door opened and they were in. He closed the door and noticed how smelly and untidy the place was. But not letting this bother him he went in and looked round. It was simple and cheap. He searched every room and then took Dummy out and sat him on the settee so he could watch. He took out a black ski mask from his pocket and slipped it over his head. Brining a wooden chair he put this in front of dummy.

Then he took a roll of duck tape from the suitcase dummy had been in, along with a blind fold. He brought these to the settee. He looked round and was about set.

"You look stupid, we had it much better organised with the fat Agent" Dummy said

"Well it didn't matter about him, he was not going to live, she is and I am not taking any chance she has a flash back or something"

Just then the door opened and in she walked, Geoff froze for a moment then headed behind the door, just as she walked in and froze as she saw the dummy looking at her. She was confused and then scared and then petrified as Geoff knocked her down from behind grabbing her hands behind her back. She was just too weak to fight back and struggle and she was confused to who it was. A thought was running through her mind Boss had ordered someone to take her out but her knees had gone to jelly already and she had no fight left in her. Her wrists where tied with the duck tape, wrapping it round several times. Then a blindfold put over her eyes and tied behind her head. Geoff lifted her up and was a little confused why she was not talking or struggling. He sat her in the chair and she was just shaking and was quiet. He went to make sure the door was locked and no one else had come back with her. He could here dummy talking as he did. When he came back in he was satisfied they were alone.

"I will only say this once, and you only have one chance" the dummy was saying.

"Please I did everything you wanted, I made the delivery all went well, please" she said confused and scared. She looked up and towards Geoff has she heard him come close.

"I want to know everything you know about that bitch with the SUV, everything do you understand, because if we get wrong answers we start cutting things off you" the dummy's voice was menacing and threatening at the same time.

"I don't understand, I did what you asked me to do" she said confused then went quiet when she suddenly realised what she had just been asked, her blood ran cold and she felt fear run down her spine and grip her very soul, the pit of her stomach felt hollow and she began to shake uncontrollably.

"Start talking, because you are going to help us one way or another" The dummy said to her.

"I don't understand, who, are you?" she said breathing heavy.

"It doesn't matter who I am, you answer the fucking questions" The dummy said still sounding cold and calculated and intimidating.

"I don't understand who you are or what you want?" she suddenly became defensive when she realised this was not who she thought it was initially.

"Tell me what you know, tell me where she goes and tell me about what she does"

"I can't tell you anything I do not know, I just work at my desk and then come home, I have nothing to do with the dealings of what goes on up stairs please this is a mistake"

"The only mistake here is the one you are going to make if you don't start fucking talking to me, if I have to start taking your fingers off I will do, if I have to slice your eye ball with a razor blade I will, do am I making myself clear, now tell me" the dummy shouted the last three words and it made her pull back on her binds, and struggle but a hand came onto her shoulder and Geoff pushed her hard back into the chair. She gasped and stopped struggling. She shook her head and started panting her words out as fear started to grip whole body and mind her like a vice slowly Appling pressure on her

"Please, I do not know anything I have only just started working there, please; they don't trust me with anything I promise you"

"Not even deliveries, you said you made the delivery" dummy said bluntly.

"Yes, no it was nothing just a drop, please it was nothing" she panicked and started to squirm on the chair and feel nauseated and uncomfortable. Geoff could see they were going to get nowhere with this so he waved to dummy to shut up.

"Listen to me, Geoff said in a calming voice. Just relax, I want you to calm down will you do that for me?" he came and stood directly in front of her.

"Who is that, what is all this about?" she said pulling back and breathing heavy again. Geoff looked around and went and got the mantle clock from the side. It was ticking away and he put it next to her so she could hear it easily.

"Listen to that clock ok, just listen the tick tock, tick tick of the clock do that for me, I want you to relax and no harm will come to you, listen to that clock and relax, listen to my voice it is all you need to hear" Geoff could see she was calming a little but nowhere near enough. He gave her a few seconds and then spoke again.

"Just listen to my voice and relax, no harm will come to you, listen to that clock sound, concentrate on it and listen to my voice. My voice is all you need" Geoff was trying to bring her under but she was too anxious and to scared. He kept going and eventually saw her relax somewhat. Her body slumped a bit and didn't look as tense. He carried on talking to her and getting her to listen to the rhythm of the clock then he started to sooth her with his voice and telling her she was feeling tired, telling her she was sleepy. Telling her to listen to him, he could see she was becoming responsive and he kept the pressure on. She eventually dropped her head and was still. Dummy looked at Geoff who looked back at it. then turned to her again and asked.

"Are you calm and want to talk to me?"

"I am calm" she said quietly and tranquilly

"Good just listen to my voice and when I clap my hands you will wake and you will remember nothing do you understand?"

"Remember nothing" she said sleepily

"Tell me what the delivery was you made"

"Young girl, been sold to client"

"The woman you work for, can you tell me about her?"

"Boss?" she said frowning

"Yes Boss, tell me about her, what do you know?"

"She is a bitch and dangerous, sells girls and boys, psychotic, hurtful, very dangerous" she started to lift her head and get agitated.

"Calm down, listen to the clock, listen to the ticking and listen to my voice" Geoff said in an attempt to calm her again, she started to nod her head down again and was still.

"Ask her where she goes is there anywhere else we can get to that bitch" Dummy said to Geoff in a low voice.

"Ok, listen can you tell me where else she lives besides her main house, is there anywhere else she goes, anywhere else she visits?" Geoff asked quietly and serenely

"I do not know" she shook her head.

"Have you ever been to her house?"

"No"

"Has she ever taken you anywhere?"

"No"

"Does she own any other properties?" Geoff was becoming inpatient.

"I do not know" she was still and totally under Geoff's spell but he was not getting anywhere and didn't like it one bit.

"Is there anyone else who can help us find out about her?"

"I don't know" was all she said and then sat still just waiting for the next question and listening to the clock. Geoff took off his ski mask and cursed.

Dummy looked up at him then said with its mouth just dropping open.

"Waste of fucking time she knows nothing, she is not as well in as we thought she was, we are just going have to use some force and some magic to get what we want"

"She is just a pawn and knows nothing dummy, even these drops she is doing we can't go there and interfere. We will have a war on our hands with some very vicious people and I do not want that, all we need is that bitch and we will have to find another way to get her"

They both agreed and could see this was a dead end, they had hoped she was involved more and knew more, but her Boss was clever and is not going to get caught that easy. It was going to have to be brute force. They took her blind fold off and the tape, they put the clock back and the chair Dummy was packed away in the suitcase and she was laid out on her settee. Geoff doubled check everything was right and they had left nothing. He walked to the door and opening it looking out, he then stepped outside and turning back he clapped his hands loudly and closed the door. Her eyes opened and she took a deep breath, she stood up and went to bed crashing out for the rest of the night.

CHAPTER SEVEN

It was Friday and Geoff was heading to his Mums for dinner, he drove and was happy it was Friday and the weekend was here again. He pulled up outside the house and glanced up to the window which had been his old room with Danny all those years ago, he went inside the house and took off his shoes. He walked into the living room and saw his sister sat with his mum on the settee talking. It was such a great thing to see, his sister actually chatting again and she even smiled big when he came she stood up and came across to him and they hugged.

His mum was very pleased and so happy she was finally coming out of her shell and back to them. It was slow at first but lately she had come along in leaps and bounds.

"How are you Geoffrey" His mum said as his sister went and sat back down with her.

"Doing good mum, he nodded towards his sister and put a thumbs sign up without her seeing and his mum nodded an enthusiastic yes too.

"That is good; me, and Cynthia are just chatting about going out shopping tomorrow"

"Really, that is great news, you two out shopping oh no it will cost dad a fortune" he smiled and was so happy to see his sister smile too. They all nodded and agreed then laughed about it. They chatted idly for a short while, until his sister went in to check on the dinner for her mum. When she did his mum leaned over and grabbed his knee saying sincerely.

"I do not know what you said to her the last time, but thank you, she has come alive again, not totally back to her old self but so, so much better. It is so good to have her come back Geoff it was horrid to see her collapse and have that break down, we will never know why or what but I am just glad it is finally coming to an end I think".

"Let's hope so mum this Family has had enough bad luck and tragedy we need happiness."

"Yes we do, and I think it is coming back to us finally, I have lost one child, I could not bear to lose another, I am so happy she is becoming responsive again" she smiled and was very happy and it showed in her eyes the way they glowed and smiled. Geoff was so delighted to see it and he was so pleased his sister was coming back to them.

It was a happy visit and he enjoyed it, even his Dad was laughing and not complaining about something. It was a great visit. After Dinner they settled down and for some unknown reason Geoff was drawn to go up and look into his old room. He excused himself and they all thought he was going to the toilet or something and were just happy Cynthia was again joining in conversations and reacting with her family again. He left them too it and walked up the stairs. The memories flooding back to him, he stopped at his old room door, then opened it and walked in. It had been stripped and very plainly redecorated but was just a spare room now with one single bed where Geoff's old beds use to be. No one used it and his parents rarely came into it anymore. Geoff sat down on the bed and looked around the room. His memories bouncing around his head, he smiled at some and frowned at others, and then he became solemn and looked sad, he remembered that night and when he changed everything.

****

Danny had been dead for over three weeks, no one had got over it, least of all Geoff, the questions had been asked, and the investigation was on going. Danny use to sleep walk when he was younger and they presumed he had done this again and fell out of the window. They took into account he had not been sleeping good and looking tired before the accident. His dad was taking counselling and was effected immensely by it, his mother too who needed medication. Geoff had told them nothing about what had happened, he just didn't think he should and that they might not believe him anyway. Also he didn't want anyone going to get the board back. He was scared and often woke up in a cold sweat in that room.

He always slept with the light on and the first week after Danny's death he would not go into the room at all. But now he was coming to terms a little with it, maybe it just was depression and he maybe was sleep walking again, maybe it was just an accident. Then this one night he was dreaming or he thinks he was dreaming. He was playing with Danny and all was great and good just like it use to be. These dreams came every night for over a week. Danny would talk to him and tell him he missed his Brother. That they should be back to how it was, Geoff was in a state of mourning and these dreams were everything to him. He longed for his little brother back; he went to bed early so to get to sleep quicker and longer so he could spend more time with Danny. He was awoke and he sat up in bed this one night, it was quiet and it was very still, there was a heavy feel to the air. But for some reason Geoff felt safe and not afraid. He listened and thought he heard a faint voice calling him. He strained his ears and turned his head towards the voice. Yes it was Danny's voice it was, calling him. Geoff looked round and tried to figure out where the voice was coming from then he looked down onto the floor. His heart missed a beat and he gasped with shock. There sat on the floor was the witch board. The wooden pointer on top of it, the board was wet and soaked, Geoff moved back onto the bed but then suddenly heard his brothers voice talking to him as if he was there with him in the same room, Geoff was confused but calmed by Danny's voice.

"Don't be afraid Geoff, it is me, Danny, don't be afraid Brother" Danny's voice said

"Danny? How, where, what is going on" Geoff was excited but also confused he sat straight up and kept looking round the room then glancing down at the board.

"Don't worry Geoff It is me, I want to come back, there is a way, will you do it?" Danny's voice was right next to him, he looked round and Eger to see his brother again.

"Yes, yes come back, yes do it come back" he said desperately.

"I can come back to my body, will you do it for me, for us we can be together again just like we use to be, you and me and I want to come back Geoff, I want out of this place, it is dark and cold and horrid" his voice became worried and Geoff could tell right away.

"Don't worry Danny I will bring you back, we can be together again, what do I do tell me"

"The Board use the board to bring me back, please Geoff, you need to use it and bring me back, please do it I don't like it here"

Geoff jumped off the bed and sat with the board he took the wooden pointer and put his finger son it then looked down at the wet and fading board.

"What do I do?" he asked"

140

"There is only one chance you only have one chance, the board will only do this once, so please Geoff bring me back" Danny's voice was becoming worried and anxious.

"What do I do Danny, Tell me what do I do?" Geoff pleaded.

The wooden pointer moved and circled under his fingers he was alarmed but didn't stop it and just went with it. He saw it move round then it started to spell out something one letter at a time he watched to see what it was.

S. A. Y. T. H. E. W. O. R. D. S.

"Say them Geoff and bring me back, tell the board you swear, and you want to bring me back, say it Geoff, please swear to the board you want me back" Danny's voice was getting agitated and also worried. Geoff took a deep breath and looked down at the board.

"I swear I want my Brother Danny back, I swear to this board I want you to bring my Brother back, bring him back I swear to you I want it"

The board did nothing for a few moments then and shook, the wooden pointer was snatched from his hand and it broke in two. The board was cracking down the centre.

"Danny what is going on?" Geoff said.

"I am coming back to my body, my body Geoff, wait, wait,, NO" Danny said fearfully

"Your, body, then Geoff gasped in horror, he shook his head and put his hand to his mouth, Danny, Danny your body?" he asked.

"Geoff what is happening where is my body Geoff?" Danny's voice screamed.

"Cremated, you were cremated" Geoff said shaking with horror

"No, buried I was buried" Danny shouted and screamed in pain and anguish.

"Danny you were Cremated" Geoff jumped as the board cracked with a snapping sound and broke in two, it lost all life and was now a useless piece wet faded wood.

All was silent, all was dead quiet, Geoff stood up and looked around his room, nothing was happening, nothing was said. He was shaking and looked down at the broken board on the floor. He breathed heavy and didn't know what to do. He sat on his bed and gulped as he looked around the room. He could not hear Danny's voice anymore. He could not feel anything and the Board was just a useless and broken and no longer had any power. Then he froze, he heard a noise, like a scratching. He looked round and then heard it again. He pinpointed it this time it was coming from the Box, the box with is Doll in it, his Ventriloquist doll. He slowly walked over and picked it up. He had not looked in here or used the doll for a very long time. He put the box on the bed and slowly opened it the doll was laid out and still. It was a lifeless piece of wood. But then to his horror he saw it twitch and eyes flash open quickly the mouth dropped and the head turned.

Geoff wanted to scream he backed off and then everything seem to be like he was walking through treacle his movement were hard and slow and his limbs seemed heavy.

"Geoff, what have you done?" Danny's voice screamed from the box.

"Danny, is that you, Danny?" Geoff was crying and didn't know what to do he couldn't move now he seemed riveted to the spot.

"My Body, this is not my Body, where is it, what have you done?" Danny's voice shouted and was sounding mad and angry. Then Geoff gasped with terror has the dummy sat up in the box its upper body lifted then just turning its head it looked straight at Geoff.

"Oh God, Geoff said holding his hand to his mouth"

"You have brought me back in this body, why, why Geoff, where is my Body?"

"Cremated" was all Geoff could say, and then broke down crying.

He told no one, and when his mum heard him talking in his room he always said he was practicing with his Dummy, which was never put back in the box. When Geoff left home the Dummy went with him and it had been with him ever since.

****

Geoff opened his eyes and the memory made him feel empty inside, he stood up from the bed and left the room. He walked back down the stairs and spent some more time with his Family the happy family who now had hope and been given the blessing of getting their daughter back to some normality and out of the horrid state of mind she had been in. Never will they know what happened and never will they know what part in it Geoff played. But then again there is much they will never know and Geoff was going to make sure it stayed that way. He wanted them happy now and they didn't deserve any more heartache or tragedy.

He left a little time later, he had made a decision and he knew someone was not going to like it. He drove steady and was home just as it was getting dark. He parked up and went into the Apartment building. When he entered his Apartment he locked the door and heading into the living room. The dummy was sat in the chair and looked at him when he walked in. None of them said anything while Geoff went to make a drink of tea. He came back and sat down on the settee and took a sip before placing it down on the floor.

"You have a good time did you?" the dummy asked unconcerned

"Yes very much so, the good news is Cynthia is coming around, she is much better and very responsive, and she is talking to everyone and even going shopping with mum tomorrow"

"Wow, let us all go out and celebrate shall we" The dummy could sense something was wrong and it knew what it was going to be.

"Stop being a sarcastic twat, it is great news and you should be very pleased" Geoff snapped

"I do not give a shit, I want us to get on with what we have planned, we need to be moving, all that with the silly cow before was stupid, and we got nowhere, we need to do this my way, your way doesn't work" the dummy snapped back louder and more argumentative .

We can't get near her, it was easy with the Agent I told you he was a, nobody this woman is powerful and she is dangerous" Geoff said raising his voice and looking straight at it.

"So am I, I can handle her and all you need to do is get me there, I will be able to take care of things, we don't even need help, so stop being a pussy and grow some balls. You are pissing me off with your lack of interest of what we have to do, you are not trying not at all just hoping it is all going to go away" the dummy snapped

"Oh shut up, she has no leverage we can use, she is powerful, has very nasty friends, and lives in a fortress. Look Cynthia is much better, she is coming back like she use to be, it is over, now leave it, we have tried and failed"

"You failed, it was a pathetic plan, you even was that scared you covered your face, why didn't you put a mask on me as well just in case" The dummy's voice had become threatening and nasty Geoff looked over and could see the body shaking with anger.

"Why don't you shut the fuck up" Geoff became angry and gritted his teeth together and tried to calm himself down, sighing out in annoyance.

"You did the fat agent ok, but after that you chickened out and are just scared, you want it all over and go back to your sad pathetic lonely life"

"At least I had a life, at least I will be alive, you don't mess with people like her, and she is to bloody powerful, she can make people disappear, she will have contacts that would come round here and I would never be seen again, No, I am not doing it any more it is over" Geoff shouted and stood up. He stormed out of the room and went to the toilet. He heard a smash on his way back in and saw the cup of tea he had made had been thrown across the room and smashed against the wall. The dummy smiling at him, then the TV wobbled and was knocked over, crashing into the coffee table and breaking onto the floor. The dummy laughed and rolled its head back. The settee lifted and was thrown over and to the side. Geoff swore and cursed and started to move towards the dummy but he was pushed back, by what, he didn't know, but some force pushed him back and off his feet. The dummy rolled its eyes and its mouth dropped open. A hideous laugh roared out and then it suddenly stopped and stared at Geoff who was getting up off the floor.

"You do this, and we get it done, I want it, and it is not over until I say it is fucking over"

Geoff looked at the dummy he had not heard it speak like this before, he swallowed and looked around, and then back at the staring eyes burning into him from the wooded head on this wooden dummy sat in the chair a few feet from him.

"It is madness, we can't do it" Geoff told it.

"Magic, that is all you need" The dummy said then looked away from him and looked down at the floor and seemed to go still and motionless.

Geoff sighed out and looked at the mess in the room; he began to clean it up, moving the settee back and shifting the TV, putting the coffee table right. He walked over and picked up the broken mug, he looked back around and saw the dummy was gone from the chair. He cleaned up the spilled tea and tidied the place back to as it was. The TV was damaged beyond repair so he trashed it out in the communal bins down by the entrance. He had a spare smaller set in his spare room and set this up. He noticed the dummy was on the floor in the bedroom he ignored it and went to watch a bit of TV before he went to bed. His thoughts were with what happened, he had never seen the dummy get that angry and demanding before, all the years they had been together and all the times they had been through never had it got that bad, not even near that stage. Everything changed when they decided to take revenge on the fat Agent after what he did to Cynthia. The dummy changed then and liked it too much; it seemed to have got a taste for it and now just wanted more. Geoff had always controlled it, always been the stronger one while the dummy had been around. But today might have been a turning point, today might have been the start of something bad and something dangerous and he knew it. No longer could he trust it, no longer could he just pretend everything is going to be alright. All these years of just existing and accepting what happened all these years living with it to the stage where it is just the norm. Well the turning point had been made and Geoff knew he had a big problem on his hands and wasn't sure how to deal with it.

It was early hours that morning while Geoff was fast asleep, he never noticed and never knew that while he was a sleep the Dummy was stood over him looking down at him, motionless, its eyes white, solid white and its head tilted to one side slightly. It stood there looking at him for a long time. Just staring and never moving an inch. When Geoff woke the next morning it was not in the room but out in its chair. He got a shower and a shave then got dressed when he came into the living room the dummy watched him moving its eyes to follow him but not its head. Geoff ignored it and made himself some breakfast. They didn't speak or interact all morning they just ignored each other. Geoff decided to go out and have a break from the place and situation. He left the place and went for a walk; he headed out across the field to the small stream beyond. He looked back when he was on his way and could see the small figure of the dummy at the widow watching him. He just carried on and had a lot of thinking to do. The fact was he had got away with murder, might be justified in some line of thought but whatever or however you look at it, murder it was. He was worried about the dummy; he had seen it change so much ever since the agent. He had lived with this dummy all these years and as strange as it was, it had always been calm and easy except when the formula was going to change, like bringing someone else into the mix. He knew he could never bring a girlfriend home the dummy would ruin it. Never had he seen the dummy react or get as upset as it is getting now though. Something had changed and he didn't like it.

Something was not right, he had to figure it out and soon, he sensed it would just get worse, he knew even if he agreed to what it wanted and kill this woman that would not be the end of it. Sitting down by the small stream on a rock he heard a little bird chirping away in a nearby bush. He listens to the gentle flow of the water and feels the warm slight breeze on his face. It was peaceful and it was quiet and it was calming. This is what he wanted in life, no rush, no worriers and no stress. He was not getting it from anywhere at the moment, his working life was stressing him out, and now his home life was doing the same. This dummy wanted to take over his life, was this dummy worth it, was it Danny or was it just a wooden dummy what really was the point. He shook his head and took a deep breath.

All these thoughts flashed through his brain and he started to get confused and perplexed by it all. All these years he had just accepted what happened, all these years he just lived with this secret, but was it time for change, was it time to let Danny go?. Looking around he tried to shake the thought from his head. The trees around him stood tall and their limbs reaching up to the sky, he looked around the area and felt good again, it was a very calming place and he liked to come here to be alone. He caught sight of a young woman walking down with her dog; she was heading down the pathway and would have to walk right past him. He watched as she came closer and thought of how it should be. How he should be able to have a girl friend, how he would like to change his life now. Why should he not be able to ask this woman out for a drink or something? Maybe they would start dating. His life would be so much different. But none of this would be possible because of the jealous streak the dummy had, always had, even growing up it always had to be his best friend and no one else was allowed to come close. He watched her come round the small fence and the dog looked at him and stopped. He smiled at it and put out his hand, it came over wagging its tail and he petted the loving animal on the head and rubbed its ears. The young woman was in her twenties and he found her very attractive. She looked nice and had a kind looking face.

"Oh sorry is he bothering you?" she said calling her dog back to her side.

"No, no not at all, I love dogs, much better than most humans to be honest"

"You are right there" she smiled at him and walked past, but slower than normal. She wanted him to start talking but he didn't, he just let her go and was disheartened about it. He watched he walk off and away. He sighed out and looked back over towards the apartment block he lived in. He could not see but he knew the dummy would be watching.

He also knew it was time for a change, his sister was on the mend, he wanted a more active and social life, he didn't want to be controlled by Danny anymore. He just had to come to terms with his brother died that night when they were young. He had to get rid of that dummy and not let it take over his life anymore. He took a deep breath and looked around him again; he tried to imagine a life with no dummy in it. How easy it would be, not as stressful he could meet someone, and he could have a fuller life. It made him feel better at first then a ping of hate came across him towards the dummy. A sense of resentment even, how it had ruined his living, run his thoughts and dictated what he had done throughout his life. The more he thought about it the more it made sense. He thought back to all the times he had not done something because of the dummy. Not had girlfriends or any friends because it got jealous. It had depressed him, compressed his life and ambition. Kept him down and just have him existing but not really living. It was time for change; he made the decision there and then. He had, had enough and was going to move on, live what life he had left for himself and not some wooden dummy. But every time he thought at about it, Danny's face came back to him. And this is what always stopped him before. But was this the time to let go, to move on, especially now the dummy had got more insane and violent. He had to do something he could not go out and try and kill this woman just because the dummy liked it. No, it was over, and no matter what that was going to be his final answer. It is over, and time to move on and start to live his live properly and get the best from it he could. No one or nothing should be able to stop him he is in control of his life and his own destiny. Talk to people get a girlfriend go out and do things, travel to places and visit countries he has never been before. This was going to be his plan. It was time for him and dummy to Part Company. Maybe he should have done it years ago maybe he should never have brought Danny back, and this is what the dummy always used against him. Well no more from now on he was in control of his own life and own decisions. It was the beginning of the rest of his life.

He stayed out and took a long walk around the outskirts of town then went up into town and had a look around the shops. He felt better about everything and was telling himself what he must do and what he is going to do. Walking back home he felt more at ease, he felt good.

It was mid afternoon when he got home, he walked in and his happier mood suddenly dropped. The place was a mess, things over turned, cups smashed on the kitchen floor where they had been thrown out of the cupboard. It looked like a bull had run through the place. He stood there and looked around. He could feel his blood boil he clenched his fist and walked into the bedroom the bed was over turned and the wardrobe was empty all his clothes on the floor. Holding his anger in, he slowly walked back into the living room, he looked around at the mess, it was a bomb site, he saw the dummy laid out face down on the floor behind the over turned settee. He stormed over to it and picked it up. He shook it and looked at its face; there was no movement or life in it at all, he shook it again.

"What the fuck have you done, why?" he shouted at the dummy shaking it has he did.

But there was no answer the dummy was still and silent, he shook it again and shouted at it.

"Answer me, what the hell is all this, why have you done it?" but still the dummy said nothing and did not move. Geoff threw it back down onto the floor. He turned the chair back over and sat down. He shook his head and looked around the place. Gathering his thought she leaned forward and put his head in his hands. He stayed there for a few minutes until he had calmed. Then he stood up and started to tidy the place back up. He could see it was more of a temper thing that had happened rather than a destructive thing. Still it had never happened before and he was pretty sure that is

154

would happen again. It didn't really take him too long to tidy and straighten the place back up. The broken crockery was thrown away and he cleaned the bit sup off the floor. He left the dummy laid out where he had dropped it. Eventually he had it back and looking more like it should, he put everything back and sat down.

"He noticed the dummy stir and then sit up, its head turn towards him. He looked at it and waited for it to speak it looked at him and the jaw dropped open. And the eyes blinked.

"You were gone for a long time" it said in a low voice.

"I will be gone for as long as I like when I like, what the hell did you do that for?"

"I couldn't really help it, something came over me, like took over me" the dummy said

"Bollocks you knew what you were doing, so don't give me any of that shit" Geoff looked away and sighed out. He leaned back in the chair closing his eyes for a few moments when he opened them the dummy was sat on the settee and looking at him.

"We have a job to get done, we have work to do" The dummy said coolly

"We have nothing to do, it is over. Can you not understand that, over no more, I am not doing anything and I want my life back, you are going to have to go" Geoff said staring at the dummy and not moving his gaze, he was furious and was standing his ground.

The jaw of the dummy snapped shut and the eyes blinked, the eye brows rose and then dropped, the lips curled and the mouth opened again, before snapping shut.

"You better not say them things, we have things to do and we have to do them OK"

"No, no, no we do not, nothing and no one is making me do anything else, and you can throw a little tantrum all you like and trash the place. It won't work" Geoff said sternly

"You need to get me to the house, I can do the rest, I can easily knockout the power the alarm and her phone then I am in and I will let you in and then we can begin" the dummy said ignoring what Geoff was saying which infuriated Geoff even more.

"Are you fucking deaf, dumb stupid or what, I am doing nothing, it's over"

"I am afraid it is not over, and won't be over until..." then dummy said then stopped

"Until what, what are you trying to say?" Geoff snapped back at it.

"It is not as simple as that is it, we have a job to do we have to go get that bitch"

"We do not have to do anything, I am sick and tired of it, I am doing nothing"

"Did you not feel it, when we killed the fat Agent, did it not give you the rush, I felt a surge and I loved it, It was like we had awakened something inside me, I was empowered I feel alive again" it sounded excited and its mouth chatted and eyes blinked over as it spoke.

"What do you mean awakened something?" Geoff suddenly got a cold feeling down his spine and looked at the over excited dummy shaking with pleasure.

"I don't know something deep inside me, it was amazing it was overwhelming I felt like I was alive and full of power and energy, I want to feel that again and you are going to help me, we are going for that bitch and I want to make it last this time" The dummy said to him.

"No, we are not, it is over, ended. We are turning a new page and moving on, I am sorry but I have a life and I want to enjoy it, I can't do that with you here" Geoff spoke quieter and with a stern but calm voice. The dummy became still and turned its head to look at him again.

"Shut up, you will do as I say, we are going for that bitch, because if we don't then I will make sure the police find out who killed the fat Agent, I can give them everything they need to come knocking on your door" the dummy's voice sounded evil, malicious and cold.

"You dirty little fuck..." Geoff started to say but the dummy butt in and stopped him.

"What are you going to say, the wooded dummy there in the corner made me do it? You going to drag Cynthia back into it, she will be destroyed you know what that will do to her, to mum and dad, you have no choice and don't you forget it Geoffrey"

"What the fuck, who the hell are you, I can just destroy you right here and right now, pull you to bits and throw you in the bin" Geoff was fuming and clenching his fists in anger.

"No you can't and will not, you brought me back I am your responsibility and your younger sibling, you can't hurt me" The dummy said apathetically.

"Oh you think so do you" Geoff started to get up but a force pushed him back down and he could not move. He tried but an unseen force seemed to have a pull on him and he could not get out of the chair. He suddenly felt scared and worried.

"You will go to prison; you know what they do to new boys in prison don't you, the whole family will be destroyed mum and dad will have breakdown, Cynthia will probably commit suicide and you will be getting ass fucked nightly inside, all because you think you can tell me what to do, we you can't tell us nothing Geoffrey not any more, I have a new friend now, An old friend actually, he reintroduced himself when we took the life of the fat Agent, he has given me more power than ever before" The Dummy smiled and closed its eyes, then opened them again and they were solid white, Geoff gasped in horror, the memory of that had never left him he had nightmares about it and hoped never to see it again. He shook his head and the look of terror and worry on his face made the dummy laugh. It laughed but in a much deeper and lower tone, like it was a different voice and person altogether.

"Danny no, please, no" Geoff pleaded.

"Danny? You think you have just been harbouring just Danny all these years" The dummy laughed out loud and it shook the very walls, it vibrated throughout Geoff's whole being he could not move his hands to put over his ears. He just had to listen to this demonic laugh.

"No, no you are dead, gone, where is Danny?" Geoff shouted, he tried to move but he just could not and it frustrated and scared him into panic.

"I am here Geoff, are you ready to listen now and stop with all this bollocks, we are together for life that was the deal, you said it, you swore to the board. Now you are going to help us and no more of your bullshit, we are going for the bitch, it makes us feel good and we like to feel good. Do you understand Geoffrey" it mocked him and stared at him waiting for an answer. Geoff breathed heavy and tried to calm down. He nodded and didn't have a choice at this time. He just could do nothing about it and had to agree, for Cynthia's sake at least.

"Good boy, now stop trying to be the macho man and do as you are told, you need to get us near the house we will get in and then you are going to help us have a night of fun and games" the dummy laughed and rocked back and forth as it did.

"Let me go out of this chair" Geoff said breathing heavy but trying to calm himself

"Not until you promise to be a good boy" The dummy made fun of him.

"Yes, alright yes" Geoff said nervously.

"Yes what?" the dummy snapped back at him

"I will help you, just let me go"

"Say please" it stared at him and waited.

"Please" Geoff said and looked back at it and regretted everything he had ever done concerning this dummy, he should have not listened all them years ago and should have left his brother dead. He was now trapped and just didn't know what to do. He knew he could tell no one, and the dummy knew he could tell no one, who would ever believe him, he would be committed. He was on his own with this, but now he knew it was not his brother sat there, it never really was. He knew from now on, he had an enemy a dangerous one; no more feeling would get in the way, he had to destroy it and that is what he was going to do.

CHAPTER EIGHT

He lived in fear of the dummy from that moment on, he didn't sleep at nights he stayed awake and dare not go to sleep, he didn't speak to the dummy unless it spoke to him and he was not eating he had lost his appetite . He took some time off work, went to the doctors and told them he had damaged his back, walking in like he couldn't move; they gave him a sick note for three week. He never had time off work so it didn't look suspicious. The plan was simple according to the dummy it was sure it could knock out her phone and alarm, then Geoff comes in and they spend the night with her in her own house locked in, where no one can hear and have some fun and games as the dummy kept jokingly putting it then laughing.

"You are annoying me with this lack of enthusiasm Geoffrey, you should be more excited and eager, I'm not liking your attitude" The dummy said sat in its own chair and looking over at Geoff who was slouched down on the settee. Looking disinterested tired and weak.

"Tough, I am not feeling well" He said feeling his eyes wanting to shut through lack of energy and sleep, of which he was not really getting either.

"That is your fault, strange you never ailed like this before isn't it. Slept like a baby every night, ate well drank fucking tea and munched biscuits all day, but look at you now"

"What do you want me to say?" Geoff complained.

"You better be ready is all I can say, go get so rest we are going in tonight and I am excited about it make sure the magic bag has what I wanted in it" the dummy dropped its jaw and blinked its eyes and shook with excitement. Geoff just turned and laid down on the settee, he was tired and it had got the better of him and his body demanded rest. He closed his eyes and within moments he was asleep and getting the much needed rest his body and mind needed.

She was ready for home and had turned off her computer, gathered her things and picked up her bag, the secretary was heading home. Or she thought she was. The phone on her desk rang, she froze and was in two minds whether to answer it, but she knew who it was and she knew the boss would see her walking across the car park and know if she ignored the call. She sighed and breathed out and answered it.

"Hello" she said trying not to show the dread in her voice.

"Get up here now" The boss shouted at her.

She put her bag down behind her desk and went up the lift to the upper floor and towards the biggest office up there. She stopped outside the door and tried to calm her nerves taking deep breaths she just hoped this was nothing serious. Then she knocked and waited.

"In" she heard the voice command.

She opened the door and walked in closing the door behind her.

"Lock it" she was ordered, she turned and with dread in her heart she locked the door. Then walked over to the large desk where the boss was looking at her up and down.

"What can I help you with Miss" she said as polite as she could with a false smile.

"Well regarding work, not a whole lot obviously, but you are not here, for your Secretary skills are you little bitch, you are here to do as you are told. I am going to have another little job I want you to do for me, same as before but this time you are driving it a lot further. You will pick up in a different place, so getting back will be by train and under no circumstances do you look in the boot is that clear?"

"Yes of course Miss, no problem, anything I can do" she said nodding her head.

"Anything you can do eh?" The Boss said looking at her with a sinful look in her eye.

"Yes" she smile nervously as she watched the Boss eye her up and down it made her feel uncomfortable and cheap in a frightening way.

"You have a boy friend?"

"No not at the moment" she answered dreading this line of talk.

"Girlfriend then" She said, enjoying making her feel uncomfortable.

"No, I am single at the moment" she smiled nervously and wished she had not done. In case it looked like she was implying something else.

"You fucking stay that way is that clear, because I want you as my little pet, and do not want anything else touching you, would you like that?" she said smirking at her.

"Err, I just want to do everything I can" she said trying to smile back and knowing what was coming she dreaded them words she had just heard and was holding back her tears.

"Strip down to your underwear, do it now I want to watch, do it slowly and do it sexy, I want you to turn me on, do you understand?"

"Yes I understand" she gulped and started to sway, she had no idea how to do this but knew the quicker she got finished here the sooner she got home, after all she knew this was part of her job when she started. She slowly undressed and watched the Boss watch her, she danced and slowly undressed, she moved well and knew how to dance she had always enjoyed dancing and loved teasing men when she was on the dance floor in night clubs. She knew how to move and look hot. But she was doing it for a woman now and was not sure what to do or show so she just hoped for the best. She watched the Boss look at her and she noticed the boss had dropped her hand down under the table. She turned and bent over taking her skirt off over her round ass. Then stepped out of it she undid her blouse and let it drop off.

She kept the movement going and was doing well to say there was no music playing but she always imagined her favourite tune playing in her head and she danced to this. The Boss seemed happy and kept staring at her. So she just carried on and stripped down to nothing, it made her feel uncomfortable but she masked it well as she danced and moved about. The Boss Stood up and came round from the table, she told her to come to her and undress her, which she did slowly. Then she felt the slap across her face and she was thrown to the ground. Both women were naked and she looked up and saw the Boss looking down at her with lust in her eye but also something else, and that something else was detestation, she detested her but she wanted her. She then pulled her up by her hair and pulled her up before slapping her again and raped her there in the office, hitting her and causing her pain as she did. Used her and abused her until she had her fill then she made her clean her up in a degrading way. All the time she knew she dare not refuse. When she had done with her she threw her out of the office naked and she had to get dressed out in the corridor luckily there was no one about to see her. She then hurried down stairs and collected her stuff and rushed to her car. She got in and quickly drove off out of the car park and away. Stopping a few minutes later by the said of the road and burst into tears, crying uncontrollably and holding her head in her hands, it had been horrible and degrading even worse than the fat Agent at least that was quick and she could control that. She had him in the palm of her hand and could make him cum without him even touching her sometimes it was easy. But this, this was a nightmare, she had no power and no dignity she was just there to be used and obviously after tonight abused too. She could still taste and smell The Boss on herself, she hated it. She took deep breaths and headed off back home she wanted a long bath and wash this smell and taste off her. Crying all the way she could see no way out of this, could she run, could she take her chances and run away?, she shook her head and threw the thought away again, she was to scared and had nowhere to go anyway, she was trapped, trapped and doomed.

The SUV was heading home less than an hour later; it had been a long day and now was early evening. She was driving home and desperately wanted to get a shower to wash the stink of that little bitch off her. She had no idea that two streets away from her house Geoff had parked his car, he was now walking towards the back of her house, it was over some green belt land and he had to be careful not to be seen. He was carrying a large suitcase. He soon got into position it was somewhere he had checked out a few days before to make sure he would have at least a bit of cover to hide. The ground was elevated so he could see over the perimeter wall. He was not at all sure about this and didn't know how dummy was going to disarm everything but he lately didn't care. He hid down behind the over grown bush, he could see the back of the house, the high fence and camera. There were other houses nearby and he had to stay hid so not to be seen by them as well.

"Can you see her?" the muffled voice said from inside the suitcase.

"No, the place is empty, no car there yet, how are you going to knock out the alarms, if you cut power the alarm will trigger anyway or just have back up power"

"Have faith and shut up" the voice commanded.

He waited and felt tired and uncomfortable, he could see out across the field behind him and across to the housing estate to his side. If anyone had seen him here then the police will be on their way by now and how would he explain it. He bowed his head down as he heard something; he looked round but had no idea what it was. He looked back up and towards the house. He was getting cold; it was dark and the chill in the air was becoming nippy. He yawned and wanted to go home. The place was going to have alarms and whatever else he was not sure about this at all. But he was suddenly noticed movement. The SUV was coming towards the place. He could see it driving down the road with the head lights on.

"Looks like she is here" He said towards the suitcase, which then flipped open by its self and Dummy sat up looked about then stood up looking over to the house. They both watched the SUV go through the electric gates and then it went out of their view. Dummy smiled and looked at Geoff. It closed its eyes and was still then flicked them open and dropped its jaw. It then hurried off; Geoff watched it disappear into the hedge and was out of sight. Then he heard the voice call to him. Five minutes then come through the gate all will be clear. Geoff didn't want to go and didn't want to be here, but he waited and looked at his watch. He waited and saw and heard nothing.

Going in the Boss locked her car then disappeared through her door. She turned off the in house sensor alarm system and went to lock the door, but she felt funny she felt faint. She shook her head and sat down on the small chair by the door. There was a load bang and she jumped and turned to see where the noise came from she dashed into the main room and could smell burning. She searched for it and followed the smell to the hallway. Under the stairs there was a fuse box and she smelt a burning coming from it. She looked around and looked at the door to make sure she had locked it. Then opened the plastic door to look into the fuses, she could smell a burning from in there, she stood up and went to get the clutch bag she had left by the front door. Searching for her phone she tried to ring but the phone was dead. She pressed it several times and tried to turn it off then on again but nothing happened. Cursing she went into the main room and found her charger and put the phone on charge. Then went to her land line phone, this was dead also which heightened her suspicion instantly. She spun round and listened to see if she could hear anyone in the house. It was silent. She ran to the kitchen and got herself a large knife from the knife rack and held it tight in her right hand. Quietly she walked from room to room searching, she was sure no one was in here because the alarm had not been triggered. Any broken window or forced entry would of set the alarm off. She knew she was safe inside. But she was going to check anyway. She checked all the rooms down stairs then went to the small computer room; this is where she had the outside TV cameras monitor. She felt a shiver when she saw this was blank.

Geoff had been waiting five minutes, he took a deep breath and was about to head off to the front gate when he heard a rustling nearby, he ducked down and saw the dummy coming back to him, laughing as it did.

"We are in, she is scared so we have begun" it said all happy and jolly.

"What have you done?" Geoff whispered still crouching down.

"The alarms are out the cameras are out and her phones are out, the SUV down, I told you I can do it, just a bit of magic, the gate is open enough to get through come on"

They both headed for the gate and Geoff reluctantly obeying, he left the suitcase there. He followed the dummy and was amazed to see the gate open about a foot, they both got through and he just hoped the cameras were out too. They dashed across the gravel driveway and towards the front door. They both got there at the same time. The dummy was laughing and Geoff was scared and shaking, he looked at the SUV, which was on its side, with dread in his heart and very soul, he didn't like all this at all.

"Now we have some fun getting in" the dummy said looking up at him.

"What do you mean, how? " Geoff said. Looking around and expecting the police or someone to come charging towards them any minute.

"You better man up, you are acting like a scared rabbit" the dummy snapped at him.

"How are you going to get in, then what do we do, how do we know she is alone?"

"She is alone, I can feel it, I am going to the back, you knock on this door and get her attention, I will slip in the back and let you in eventually wait until I do, if she comes out you take her down, is that understood" it ordered him, then the dummy shook with excitement and headed off around the house without saying another thing.

"Fuck" Geoff said looking around again, he didn't want to be here and took a deep breath and then knocked on the door.

She jumped as she heard the knock, she knew there was something wrong, and something was not good here. She held the knife in her hand and was not afraid to use it. She edged towards the front door. It was a solid heavy wooden door and she knew it was pretty secure. She looked out of the spy hole but could see no one. She listened and tried to hear who it was. But there was no sound coming from outside. She took a deep breath and sighed out. She looked round and went into the living room again to check her phone she had put on charge. Looking at it she cursed and saw it was still dead. The smashing sound from the back made her heart jump. Fear finally gripped her. She looked about and didn't know what to do at first. The glass breaking was obviously a window being smashed. How the hell could her phones be dead, the cameras not working, the alarm system down? She gathered her nerve and went for it, she dashed to the rear and to the kitchen she was revved up and ready to stab anyone she came across. The window was broken but it was a small one, not really big enough for a grown man to get through. She went and checked the back door, it was locked. Was something thrown through, she thought but she could see nothing just broken glass. She suddenly became very scared and looked round, what has come in through there, is there someone in the house, but the window is too small. She gritted her teeth through her fear and was not going to have anyone trying to frighten her, she was going to use this knife and make them pay. She headed back into the main room and heard footsteps but light ones running across the wooded floor by the hallway. She dashed out but could see no one. She gripped the knife and her knuckles went white. She edged into the living room and was shocked into stopping in her tracks, sat in the leather chair was a dummy, a ventriloquist doll. It was limp and just sat there. She looked round and started to breath heavy, she walked into the room and jumped as the door slammed shut behind her. She instantly went to try and open it.

But it was stuck solid, she looked over to the second exit but this door was slammed shut too. She screamed as the dummy lifted its head and looked at her. It dropped open its jaw and then snapped it shut staring at her and watching her as she slowly circled round, she turned and dashed for the door trying desperately to open it but it would not move it was closed and would not budge. The dummy laughed and she screamed out in fear at the sound of the demonic laugh that came from the wooden doll. She struggled with the door and pulling at the handle she hurt her fingers and broke her expensive nails, but she didn't care.

"Sit down bitch" the dummy said

She carried on fighting to open the door, and then she gasped with fear as unseen forces seem to hit her hard and she fell from the door and onto the floor dropping the knife as she did. Her head was ringing with pain and she looked over at the dummy staring at her with dead eyes. She had never seed so scared in her life, she had seen and done a lot, but this was making her petrified to her bones, she was shaking and didn't know what to do.

"I said sit down" the dummy shouted in anger at her and she again was thrown by an unseen force towards the leather couch. She scrambled up and sat on the couch looking at this demonic doll that was in her house and talking to her, she shook her head and could not believe it, none of this was happening surely she was dreaming. The doll raised its eye brows and smiled a hideous smile at her, then shook and chuckled to its self. She looked round and wondered if someone was controlling the doll from somewhere else. She could not understand why she was being thrown about when there was nothing here; some force was moving her, some unseen energy. She started to get her wits back her nerve, the initial shock of it all was over. She looked around there must be someone somewhere controlling the doll.

"What are you looking for bitch?" the doll asked her.

"Who is this, what the hell do you want?" she said looking round and trying to figure out what was happening and how it was happening.

"Well we are here to play a few games, to see if you can take a bit of pain and no doubt your own medicine." The dummy told her and getting annoyed she was not looking at him.

"Games, what the hell are you talking about, who is this, show yourselves"

"I'm here stupid bitch, here, it's me" The dummy shouted at her, and leaning forward in the chair to get her attention. She slowly looked at the doll and tried to see how it was working.

"What do you want, who are you?" she said again.

"I told you, I am here to have some fun, I know about your little game on the side, selling girls and boys. You make a lot of money out of it don't you; this advertising job you do it's all a front isn't it. I know a lot about you and the drop off's you arrange"

She thought for a moment and then cursed under her breath, she brought the Secretary in and suddenly this happens, she made a mental note to have her erased.

"So what do you want, money?" she asked leaning back on the couch, knowing this dummy was just a front someone somewhere was behind it.

"No I do not want money, I want to make you suffer that is what makes me happy"

"Oh is it now, well you have no idea who you are messing with here, I have some very, and I mean very powerful friends, they will make you and anyone you have with you disappear, then they will do the same with you entire family" she sighed out and looked at the doll, thinking it had some sort of camera in it so she was talking to someone on the other side.

"And you have no idea who you are messing with either, I do not need powerful friends I am powerful enough as you will see. You think you are going to get out of this think again"

"Well let's cut the crap, what is it you want and how did you get in here and past my security system?" she suddenly realised and again looked around the room.

"I think you do not realise what is happening, I see you brought a large knife in here, was that for me?" the dummy said looking down at the knife on the carpet where she had dropped it.

"It will be for whoever is behind this, why don't you show yourself instead of hiding behind a fucking doll" she snapped out sharply and loudly.

"Maybe it's the fucking doll that is doing all this, there is no one behind me" it smiled.

"I've had enough of this shit" she stood up and came for the doll, but it looked at her and she was thrown back violently onto the couch. She cried out and had no idea what he thrown her here. She scrambled up and looked over at the laughing dummy. She sat back down on the couch and again tried to calm herself, there must be a perfectly simple logical explanation to all this. How is she being thrown about like this? She was confused and suddenly dashed for the door again. But it was still locked and she could not get out. The dummy just sat watching her and laughing then its eyes opened wider and things started to move across the room and hurl through the air at her. Ornaments, picture frames, a small table. The dummy laughed uncontrollably as she dodged and tried to get out of the way of the flying objects coming towards her. They smashed to pieces as they hit the wall and door, all round her. She covered her head with her arms and hands and ducked back down to the floor. Then scrambled across the room to get out of the way, she stood up and looked at the dummy smiling at her. She was shaking now and the confusion and anger she had was turning again to her original fear. She stood silent and still looking down at this wooden doll that was terrorising her and she couldn't comprehend it but for now had to accept it. She was breathing heavy and slowly eventually she turned and sat back down on the couch. The dummy dropped open its bottom jaw, and blinked its eyes and then stared at her again snapping the jaw shut.

Geoff was still outside and getting cold, he had heard nothing else and was getting nervous, he had no idea what was going on and didn't really want to know. The thought of just going home and leaving the dummy to it had crossed his mind but he decided against it. He stomped his feet and blew into his cupped hands for a little warmth. He was by the side of the house and out of sight at least but close enough he could hear if the front door opened.

"Look what the hell do you want, I do not know who you are or how you are doing these fucking tricks but let's stop fucking about and tell me what you are after" She said not understanding or comprehending the situation. Rather she was too stubborn, narcissistic or just ignorant but she had already had enough.

"I am here for revenge for all the innocents you have fucked up" the dummy said to her turning its head to the side as it did.

"I do not know what the hell you are on about, I run an advertising agency and that is it, is it money you are after, what do you want, you have the wrong person" she said dully.

"You had dealings with the fat Agent, he was your friend we saw you with him a few times, he no doubt supplied you a few girls along the way eh?" the dummy smiled and blinked slowly as it saw her face change and she shifted in her seat. It started to chuckle as it notice her face turn white and the blood drain from her. She suddenly was scared and looked around once again but knew the door would be locked so thought against it. She didn't want any more things thrown at her or to be violently hit to the ground again.

"Ok, so what is it you want from me?" she said trying to sound calm and hide her fear.

"Why do you keep asking me the same fucking question?" the dummy snapped.

"Answer me, what is it you want, Money?" she raised her voice and the dummy sensed the slight quiver in it, she was holding to together well but she was beginning to crack.

The dummy looked at the knife then it looked back at her, it stared at her she felt strange, she felt heavy and suddenly could not move she was stuck. No matter how much she tried she could not move a muscle. It scared her and she breathed very fast and heavy. She could move her eye and speak but otherwise she was paralysed from the neck down.

"We are going to play a little game you and me, you see, you will do anything and everything I want, you will have no choice. I am going to ask a question if you get it right all good. If you get it wrong something has to come off" the dummy smiled at her and then the knife as if my magic flew off the ground and landed in the arm of the chair next to her. She whimpered and looked at it but as much as she tried she could not move.

"Please stop, I will give you anything you want what is it you want?" she pleaded.

"I have a lot of tricks I can do, watch this." The dummy said ignoring her

She felt her right arm move but she was not in control of it, she pulled out the knife from the arm of the couch with her right hand and then her left hand moved and spread her fingers on the arm of the couch. She watched in horror as she was being controlled and could do nothing about it, it was all against her will. She put the blade of the knife across her little finger, facing away from her hand and held it there. She was sweating and her whole face was shaking and she started to mumble something.

"Ok let me see, I can't help but notice you are a very attractive woman, very fit and healthy body. Let's have a look" the dummy smiled and dropped its jaw open looking at her legs as they opened and she could do nothing about it. She was stuck there with legs wide open sat in front of this dummy and she was horrified and looked down at the knife she was holding across her little finger, holding but having no control over.

"Oh very nice, no underwear, you ever been fucked by a wooden dummy before"

She breathed out and could not speak the fear had her in a pincer grip and she was in panic now, sweating and her eyes full of fear. The dummy rolled its head back and started to laugh out loud and the laugh turned from a mid pitch to a low more growling tone, as if someone suddenly had taken over the laugh. It rolled about and then shifted in the seat. Looking at her the eyes had suddenly turned white. She gasped and started to cry, looking down at the knife then back at the white eyes looking at her. They turned back as she stared at them and the dummy seemed to settle again.

"Ok, let's see, yes this is how it goes, I ask you a question, if you give me a wrong answer you cut your finger off. So you have five chances on that hand, then if we need to we can go to the toes and then other bits, fond of your nipples and tits are you?"

"Please, I can give you anything you want" she nervously and fearfully said.

"I wonder how many times young girls have said that and you just laughed at them, sold them on to perverted Bastards, knowing damn well what is going to happen to them"

"No, look I have money I can make you rich" she said her head shaking

"What will I do with money I am a wooden dummy" it said seriously and waited for an answer, that didn't come until for at least a minute.

"Please tell me what you want" she pleaded with the dummy sat looking at her.

"Did you know a girl called Cynthia, the fat agent molested and raped her, was you going to take her and sell her for him?"

"No, I have never heard of her, the agent as you call him was just someone... "She screamed before she could finish her sentence. She looked down in horror as she pushed the knife down across her own finger and cut it off. The small finger fell to the floor and the blood oozed out.

The dummy shook its head and sighed out looking disappointed before calmly saying

"One down four to go on that hand. Do I have to ask you again, because this is going to hurt you much more than me" it laughed again and the jaw dropped open several times as it did.

"I had nothing going like that, no Cynthia, I did not know anyone of that name" she shouted looking down at her hand with horror. The blood was coming out a lot and she screamed as her hand came up and repositioned the knife on her next finger. She tried but still could not move she was at the total mercy of this wooden dummy sat in front of her.

"I think you are lying, but I will give you the benefit of the doubt, so tell me, what was your relationship, with that fat obnoxious Bastard" the dummy asked solemnly

"I knew him through the agency, that is all, he had clients and sometimes we did some advertising work for him that was it, nothing more" she screamed again as the second finger was cut off and feel to the floor joining the other one.

"You are not even a good liar, don't take me for an idiot, I might be made out of wood and look like it but I am no dummy" it laughed again and she could tell whoever it was, was enjoying every minute of this torture.

"Alright, alright yes he groomed some girls, but I swear I know nothing of any Cynthia, I would tell you if I did" she shouted in panic and desperation.

"That's better, see much easier on your fingers isn't it when you tell me the truth, so did you ever use any of these girls yourself, did you watch any of the sick Bastards use them"

"No, I swear" she screamed and sobbed as she cut her third finger off, the loss of blood was making feel weak and she started to sob out loud and pleaded over and over. But it all fell on deaf ears, and the dummy just revelled in her anguish and enjoyed it immensely.

"I think we will start on your face, how about an ear, or your nose, or stab your eye out, cut your eye ball open, maybe your tongue so you can't tell me any more lies" The dummy finally said after watching her suffer for a few minutes.

"Please, let me go, I will give you anything" she pleaded, she was scared now and the worry and trepidation had taken over her completely. She looked at the dummy and didn't understand how all this was happening, how she could be stuck and not able to move. How she was being made to do these things. All she knew was she was in danger and a lot of trouble she was helpless to get away from.

"Well you might start to bore me so let's play a new game; it's called, open your mouth and let's see how fucking far we can force this knife down your throat shall we"

"No, no please I will answer anything you want, please" she said frantically. The dummy moved off the chair and stood up, her eyes widened as it walked towards her; she shook her head in disbelief it stood in front of her and bent down turning its head to look under her skirt. Then lifted its head back up, smiling at her. She shook her head and started to panic. The dummy smiled and looked again and moved closer. It looked her all over and came close to her almost touching her but not quite.

"You think you are something really special don't you?" it said with hate in its voice

"No, no I am not, no" she said shaking her head.

"I know you are not, that is not what I said I said you think you are" The dummy condescended and stared her in the eye coming close to her face.

"Please, just let me go, I will, I can give you anything you want" she started to cry and the tears fell down her cheeks and rolled off her chin.

"I wonder how many times you have seen girls cry, and you just watched them and did nothing, I bet you enjoy it, the power the sense of all important don't you" the dummy's voice was venomous and full of hate. It backed up and looked at her tilting its head to the side and it seemed to be studying her for a short while.

"What can I do to make this stop?" she said her voice quivering and broken.

"Die in a way that makes me happy, you have no idea the pain and suffering you have caused in your fucking horrid life, you are going to get a little taste of it now, all fucking night long, at least maybe into tomorrow as well we will see how much you can take or if I just get bored with you" the dummy looked at her and just stared, it made her nervous and it enjoyed seeing the panic and the fear in her eyes.

"Who are you?" she shouted in desperation.

"I am just a piece of wood doing a job, a hard working kind of bloke, a good old stick you know" it laughed out loud and its head wobbled in the socket on the shoulders. She cried out and shook her head, crying even more. The dummy bent down again and looked up between her legs.

"Nice, clean and smooth, I have a friend who might want a piece of that I will just go get him" the dummy walked across the room, the door opening by its self before it got to it. She tried more and more but could not move she was totally paralysed. She heard the front door opening, and then she heard voices, the front door slam shut again. And it seemed two people were having an argument or something outside in the hall, she could not make out every word but they were there just outside the room door. She could smell the burning she smelt before only now it seemed stronger; it was like an electrical smell of burning wire, she was not sure what it was but it didn't smell or look good and it just added to her fear and nervous state.

Geoff didn't want to come into the room he didn't want any more part of it, but he could see the dummy getting angrier and more volatile with him.

"Look just imagine what she could of and would of done to Cynthia, I have her just were we need her, I want her to feel the pain and t e helplessness of her victims. I am bored now with what I am doing. I want you go in there and fuck the bitch. Make her feel helpless and used and petrified just like the young girls she has sold, come on" the dummy shouted and shook with anger as Geoff backed off and shook his head.

"Listen I don't want no more part of this, and what is that smell?" Geoff said looking round as the smell got stronger and he tried to figure out where it was coming from.

"Who cares, now listen to me you spineless piece of shit, just remember what I said, and just remember what it will be like when you are in prison and mum and dad broken beyond repair, Cynthia in a psychiatric ward. You want all that do you, you are in this up to your fucking neck so stop pissing me off and let's get going, there is a bitch to roast" the dummy walked towards the room door and turned looking at Geoff. Who shook his head, but walked towards the door. He knew he had no choice at this time but he was concerned about the electrical smell, it was very strong. He went into the room and they were both gone out of the hallway. If they had stopped a few seconds more they might of noticed the smoke coming from the under the stairs where the fuse box was on fire.

And the under part of the wooded stairs was burning out of control the smoke had risen up and filled the upstairs rooms already.

"Look I have brought a friend, someone who is going to fuck you every which way, because he has not been fucked before so he should be able to manage it I would say" the dummy announces as it walked into the room. Geoff followed and the door slammed shut behind him by its self. He looked at the woman sat on the couch petrified and bleeding from her hand, she was holding a knife over her third finger and Geoff deduced she had cut her own fingers off helpless to resist. The dummy walked up to the woman and stood in front of her. It looked her in the eye and grew pleasure from the fear it saw. She shook her head and looked away. She noticed Geoff walking round into her field of vision.

He walked in front of her, and could see the sheer terror on her face, her hand bleeding and the obvious anguish and pain in her eyes, she was on the verge of total breakdown.

"Watch this, it is so good and funny" the dummy said to Geoff it went and sat back down on the chair and looked at the knife for a moment. It wobbled in her hand and she lifted it up to her face rubbing the blade across her face she cried out but could not stop it, she had no control over her own actions. Placing the sharp end of the blade under her ear she stopped.

"Stop this, stop it now, it's enough I think she gets the message" Geoff futilely said knowing it was useless and pointless to talk and try and reason with it

"Oh no, this is the fun bit she is going to ask you to fuck her now, and it better be convincing or she will cut her own ear off" the dummy laughed out loud and rolled back in the chair.

"Stop it, I am not going to fuck her anyway" Geoff said regretting he could not come up with something better to say and cursing under his breath.

"You will do exactly what I want and so will she" the voice came out of the Dummy but was the low growling one again, the eyes had flicked white. The woman screamed and tried to move her head away from the knife under her ear but could not. Geoff looked at the dummy and knew it no longer was Danny, was it ever Danny? He asked himself the question again, he had been asking it to himself more and more.

"Stop this, let us just calm down" he said putting his hands up in front of him and walking towards the dummy. He felt a savage invisible hit to his head it reeled him back and he curled up on the floor in pain. He was dazed and shook his head and looked over from the ground. He could see the woman and she screamed as she sliced her own ear off with the knife. He watched it drop to the floor and the blood followed.

"No" she shouted out and pleaded in tears, she watched in absolute horror as she cut her remaining fingers off her right hand, finishing with her thumb. She hacked at them and cut them with the knife. The dummy watched this sadistic site with glee. The eyes were white the voice was a low growl as it laughed watching the blood soak into the carpet. Geoff shook his head to clear the dull ache and blurred vision. He could smell the smoke coming from under the door. He stayed low for a moment and thought about what to do.

"So what is next, your other ear, or if lover boy down there can't get it up how about you fuck yourself with that blade, that will be lovely and messy" the dummy sounded what it had become, insane and sadistic. The eyes stayed white all the time and the voice was stuck low and growling. It laughed at the panic and horror in the woman's face as she moved the knife down and between her knees. Geoff knew there was no Danny left, even if there had been once there was not now, he thought how he could get out but he knew he needed to do more, this dummy had to be destroyed and it would never leave him alone if he didn't destroy it now, here tonight. He had to play it along, but could he convince it? He knew he could not, it would see his fear and false facade straight away.

"What about you lover boy, you want to see this bitch fuck herself with a blade?" Geoff stood up still a bit wobbling and came over. He looked down at the dummy looking at the woman wide eyed and smiling.

"If you do that it will be over too quick, she will be dead, then the fun stops" Geoff said hoping he had said it convincingly. The dummy stayed quiet for a moment then slowly turned its head to look at him.

"Aw, look at you trying to be all hard and un concerning, you forget soft boy, I have lived with you for many years I know exactly what you are capable of, I must say you did surprise me with the agent mind you, so hope for you yet." the dummy said looking up at him stood there trying not to shake with nervous tension.

"Well there is a lot you don't know about me" Geoff said glancing over at the woman who was sweating, crying and her head shaking as she looked at the knife in her own hand between her legs, she knew at any moment it could be thrust up inside her repeatedly. The loss of blood was making her feel sick and weak, but she concentrated on the knife at all times. Geoff saw the blood dripping off her chin from her ear severance, he saw the left hand fingerless and the carpet soaked with blood. He tried to look disinterested.

"So what would you suggest, we have all night after all, sure you don't want to sample that hole, any hole for that matter she can't resist" The dummy growled and giggled.

"Why don't you get the names and address for her associates" Geoff suggested.

"We can pay them a visit too, have a party like this every night, now wouldn't that be a thing, but I don't think so" the dummy said then shook its head.

"Well after this what is there to do?" Geoff sat down next to the woman on the couch. He tried very hard not to be disturbed by all this and wasn't sure he was doing a good job. But he had to try something. He could smell the smoke now and knew there was a fire somewhere in the house. If it could be seen from outside someone would have phoned the fire brigade and they would be on their way. He didn't want to be here if and when they arrived. His other problem was this woman has now seen his face. She knew who he was, he didn't like the situation and he was becoming desperate. And ready to try anything, he could feel his knees going to jelly and the empty pit in his stomach where the butterflies were dancing.

"After this, you think there is an after this?" the dummy looked at him and it didn't move it just stayed stationary and glared at him.

"So what is the plan?" he asked getting more and more nervous as he did.

"You sleep like a woman do you know that, all curled up and safe in your bed, I have often thought about strangling you in your sleep do you know that" the dummy said coldly.

"Why didn't you. Where is Danny?" Geoff asked he was becoming more and more nervous and the dummy could feel it and sense it with ease.

"Because I have plans for you and your precious little sister, she looks juicy" the dummy smiled at him and then laughed.

"She has nothing to do with all this" Geoff defended the best he could

"Stupid, of course she does, she started it all remember, the fat agent, who groomed her, got her drunk, molested and fucked her did whatever he wanted, I wonder what he did by the way, has she ever told you" The dummy smiled at him and laughed at his discomfort.

"Just leave her out of this, it's just you and me, always has been"

"Oh no not just you and me, there has always been another" it jaw dropped open and it laughed out loud with its deep growling hideous laugh.

Before Geoff could say anything the woman had plunged the knife between her legs and screamed out with an agonising pain and anguish and fear all combined in that one moment, that one scream. She pulled the blood soaked knife out and plunged it in again. Geoff stood up and backed off he found the whole thing sick and insane, she could not stop herself and soon she was limp, blood oozed out over her hand and couch dripping onto the floor. She was dead bled to death, and the knife was stuck where she had plunged it in deep, her body went limp and she slumped back into the couch.

"What the fuck, no" Geoff backed off but not too much.

"Well that was disappointing and anticlimactic" the dummy laughed and has it did it rocked its head back, Geoff kicked the head as hard as he could it flew off and out of the body. It landed across the room and the body fell to the deck. He plucked up all his courage and took the knife from where it was sticking out of the woman. It was warm and covered with blood. He dashed over to where the head had landed but to his horror it was not there. He raced back to the dummy's body and saw the head rolling towards it. He ran and kicked the head again. Maybe if he could keep them separate they would not be able to work. This idea was short lived has he was picked up in the air and invisibly thrown across the room. He dropped the knife and painfully crashed into the door. He could see the head rolling again across towards the body. He could feel the heat on the door and knew there were flames on the other side. He mustered up all his strength and ran for the body of the dummy he rolled up and grabbed it. Scrambling back towards the door he tried to open it but burnt his hand on the handle. Suddenly to his surprise and horror the body of the dummy he had in his hands started to kick and punch at him, trying to grab him around the throat. He bashed it against the wall.

Then throwing it across the room he saw the knife coming through the air towards him. He had to duck as it only just missed him and stuck in the door. He rolled away and coughed as the smoke came under the door and started to fill the room. He was disorientated and looked around his eyes beginning to water. He couldn't see anything and ran for the other door. Luckily it opened but he was hit by a wall of smoke and flames, he backed off back into the room and looked around for something to help him. He rushed over to the window coughing he was losing any strength he had. He tried to open the window but it was locked. He didn't have the strength to smash it. Smoke was filling the room and he found it hard to see through it. The room was catching fire fast and the flames moving swiftly over everything and igniting what they touched and within seconds it was an inferno. He felt the heat burn his skin he was desperate and scared and weakened. Then he noticed the open door break off its hinges and push through the air out towards the fire. Instinctively he followed he caught sight of the dummy dashing away as the flames came back around the door that had been used as a shield. Heading out towards the back he held his hand to his mouth and fought his way through the smoke and flames and banged into the back door. He noticed the small window broken and air coming in, he bent down and took some much needed lung full's of air. He looked up and to his horror the sight of the burning dummy walking towards him; arms outstretched the eyes white and the growl on its face. It looked demented and demonic. It was burning and the clothes had gone its hair alight and it was just the bare wooden dummy moving towards him. He was powerless to defend himself the smoke had made him weak and his eyes were watering. He thought this was it, he slumped down and looked at the white eyes staring at him and the dummy moving forward, he became stiff and his muscles became solid he couldn't move. His body was lifting off the ground by about six inches he was suspended in mid air and he was helpless and could not resist if he wanted too. The dummy started to laugh, that deep growl of a laugh and he could see it was getting closer and closer this was the end. This is how he was going to die, his life suddenly flashed before him, his Parents his sister, his whole life and Danny. But suddenly he fell to the floor with a thud as if the power that was holding him was severed. The dummy shook and shook its head cursing and trying to resist something, it was being pulled back and it cried out. Struggling frantically and burning up as it did. Geoff didn't know what was happening, it looked like something was pulling the dummy back and away from him, he heard the cry and the dummy trying to fight but it was struggling and burning even more now, the figure was alight and it moved back against its will, its feet sliding on the ground, it was struggling but it was not winning this fight and something was pulling it back into the house into the flames.

"Run" Geoff heard the voice shout, it bellowed throughout the house like a loud rumbling presence, the voice he recognised as his brother, his twin brother Danny was shouting at him to run. He found strength in this voice strength to get out he moved around and got some more air from the broken window, filling his lungs and coughing. He looked back and could see the dummy fighting it seemed to be struggling with some unseen entity and Geoff knew what it was. The noise of anger and frustration and pain all filled the place as the dummy screamed and was dragged back into the flames. It was struggling and fighting and shaking with anger as it was dragged back. The wooded part of the doll were falling to bits the wood caught fire and was burning away it fell and was laid on the floor the head still looking at Geoff. The body just about gone

197

and turned to ash the head blazing and on fire savagely, the eyes turned from white to red, then back to normal.

"Run, Geoff run" was the last thing the dummy's head said the jaw dropping open for the last time as the whole head was gone and engulfed, flames coming out of the mouth and eye sockets the hair was burnt off already and the head alight crackling and burning away. Nothing would be left it would be gone and without a trace.

Geoff held his breath and stood up and fought with the locks to undo the back door, his eyes were watering and he struggled to see but he managed it eventually. The flames had engulfed the house now and it was an inferno. The heat was intense and the flames savage as they eat and destroyed everything. He pulled the door open and fell out onto the back garden gasping for air as he did. He heard the sirens in the distance and knew he had to get away. He scrambled to his feet and tried to get his bearings, he still had the worry of people seeing him running away, he headed towards the gate and off away through the open field and ground. He ran and kept running. He coughed and his lungs hurt badly, they were tearing up as he breathed and eventually he had to stop. He couldn't run any more. He coughed and took in deep breaths of air. He could see the house was ablaze and the blue flashing lights approaching. People were looking out of their windows and coming out onto the street. He rested for a little while just to get his breathing back to some normality. He watched the house burn intensely and knew nothing would be left, smoke bellowed up into the night sky and the flames lit up the surrounding houses. People were shouting and some women screaming there was panic on the street. He coughed and breathed deep and tried to calm himself, his lungs were burning and hurt when he inhaled. He was shaking and was scared; he had no idea what to do about all this. He eventually headed back to his car several streets away being very careful not to be seen. More people were looking towards the fire then to notice him getting into his car and driving away down the road. He coughed and the pain ripped into his lungs. He wiped his eyes where they had been watering he tried to stop shaking and he tried to concentrate on his driving and the road ahead. He missed a breath as a police car came racing towards him with its lights flashing and siren blowing, it sped past him and he watching it go in his rear view mirror. Sighing out nervously, he swallowed and coughed again. He was still shaking and his eyes were sore just like his throat. He didn't want to think what he looked like, it must have been a desperate state, and he just wanted to get away for this place and try and leave it all behind. He thought about Danny about what had happened. He felt the tears dwell up in his eyes, was it from the smoke and fire or something else. He sniffed up and coughed again. Driving steady now he was making good distance, he could not hear the commotion anymore and didn't look back. He just wanted to get home and lock the door.

CHAPTER NINE

He had no idea what really had happened to the dummy, he suddenly had a sinking feeling as he drove in case it was in the car. He saw it burn and perish in the flames but still the fear rose in him, he pulled up by the side of the road and looked around inside the car and then went out to check in the boot. But there was nothing, he slowly knelt down and looked under it as well. He was relived there was still nothing to see. He knew what he heard; it was Danny's voice, his real voice the voice of his brother when he was his brother and not some dummy. He drove home quickly and parked up. He looked around to make sure there was no one about. He locked up the car and ran in; he stripped and put all his clothes in a plastic bag tying it shut air tight after. He then went and got a shower, he washed the smell of the smoke of himself. He still was coughing and his chest hurt from it. He stayed in the shower a long time washing his body and his hair several times. Eventually he came out and made sure his door was locked. He walked into his apartment and it was just as he had left it earlier that evening. He was still on edge, and all the usual doubts and questions were going thought his head. What if he had been see, what would he say if the police came, what if the dummy was not dead, what if it reported him, What if it came back, what if it did what it said it was going to do to him and his family. He shook his head and sat down; he put his hand out in front of him and saw it was shaking like a leaf. Taking deep breaths he calmed himself somewhat and went to make a cup of tea and a sandwich. He looked out of the window and up the street while he did, still nervous and still expecting the police or someone coming down after him. After he had finished and washed the pots he came and sat down on the settee again. Glancing across at the chair where dummy use to sit. He picked up the TV remote and put the Television on. A talent show was on as he watched a man walked onto the stage with a ventriloquist doll smiling and starting his act. Geoff looked at the doll and quickly turned off the TV. He got up and checked the door was locked again. Then he went to bed and tried to sleep but he knew he wouldn't be able to, he lay on his back looking at the ceiling and every time he closed his eyes he saw the dummy with white eyes looking at him, he opened his eyes with a start and just lay there all night breathing heavy from the smoke and coughing most of the time. His lungs burned and he hoped there was no real damage.

The next day he was out of bed early, he had already looked out of the window a dozen times; he was expecting the police to call at any moment. What if he had been seen or his car reported being parked there. He made himself a big breakfast; he was very hungry and had not eaten right for over a week. He did enjoy his food and while he was washing up his plate he kept an eye on the road. He went out and threw the plastic bag with his clothes in; into the rubbish bins covering them so no one could see it on top. Staying the house for the next two days he did the same routine of looking out of the window every ten minutes or when he heard a car pull up outside. His nerves were becoming shot and he couldn't sleep. But by the third day he thought maybe his car was not seen after all, they would of had the address my now. There was nothing to actually connect him with this woman. The doll must of perished in the fire, it was wooden so there would be nothing left of it, even if there were it shouldn't lift any suspicion. Danny was gone, but strangely he felt nothing and no regret, he kept seeing the doll with white eyes not Danny at all. But he still heard Danny's voice that voice telling him to run will be with him for the rest of his life. Maybe just maybe he was safe. He watched out of the window and the dustbin men came and emptied the bins. It made him feel a little better knowing the clothes were gone. He sighed and decided to go for a walk. He had not been out of the house since, so wanted to get some air. He went down the field by his apartment and down to the little stream; he sat there like before when he saw the girl with the dog. He was hoping she would come past again. But she didn't, he sat there taking in some deep breaths of fresh air. His lungs felt better today but still a little sore. Eventually he headed back and got something to eat. He felt better each day that passed. But he would never be the same again he knew that. The week he went back to work was a long and hard one he just didn't want to be there, it was Friday he had done his shopping and also visited his parents house for tea. He came home locked the door put everything away and settled down and watched a bit of TV, he sat on the settee and glanced over at the chair Dummy use to sit, he had not used in it himself since. He yawned and turned the TV off and left the room brushed his teeth and went to bed. It had been along week and he was glad it was over. It was not long before he was asleep. The apartment was quiet, still and all seemed well, nothing had happened since that night and he was trying to put it all behind him. The apartment was silent and dark. Then the Television flickered on by its self.

The End.

Other titles by the same author

THE PARA

THE LAKE

SECOND CHANCE

BROKEN

HIDDEN DARKNESS

BROTHERHOOD THE PARA 2

LUGHOLE AND THE YORKSHIRE MICE

Printed in Great Britain
by Amazon

10483970R00119